A Waste of Shame
and Other Sad Tales of
the Appalachian
Foothills

By

Geoffrey Smagacz

Wiseblood Books

Milwaukee, Wisconsin

Map of Appalachia used by permission of
Sparkman + Associates, Inc., Bristow, VA.

Printed in the United States of America
Set in Arabic Typesetting

Library of Congress Cataloging-in-Publication Data
Smagacz, Geoffrey, 1957-
A Waste of Shame
and Other Sad Tales of
the Appalachian Foothills/ Geoffrey Smagacz;
1. Smagacz, Geoffrey, 1957-
2. Fiction

ISBN-13: 978-0615879659
ISBN-10: 0615879659

APPALACHIA

TABLE OF CONTENTS

Acknowledgements

I am deeply grateful to Gotham Writers Workshop, novelist Lisa Reardon, Anthony Call, Lisa Martinez, Dr. Calvin Smith, Helen Hubartt, Deborah Gray, Laura Perry and Joshua Hren for their input and suggestions. I would also like to thank the editors of the following publications for kindly publishing many of the stories in this collection.

"Shooting Practice," (Chapter 1) *The Other Herald*, Issue 53, Summer 2012, pp. 15-19

"The Broken Globe," (Chapter 7) *East Of The Web*, Eastoftheweb.com, 2011.

"Bull Derby," *Leaf Garden*, Issue #10, August, 2010, p. 30.

"What Happened To Gary Lee," *Leaf Garden*, Issue #10, August, 2010, pp. 28-29.

"Agnes," *Skyline Review*, Walter Forest Press, Third Edition, 2011, pp. 161-164.

"Drawing Fishes," *Dappled Things*, Volume 5, Issue 2, 2010, pp. 76-79.

"The World Is Too Much With Us," *Title Goes Here*, Issue 10, January 2012, pp. 29-31.

"You Will Know Happiness" *Title Goes Here*, Issue 10, January 2012, pp. 29-31.

For my parents, Walter and Susan

CXXIX

The expense of spirit in a waste of shame
Is lust in action; and till action, lust
Is perjur'd, murderous, bloody, full of blame,
Savage, extreme, rude, cruel, not to trust;
Enjoy'd no sooner, but despised straight,
Past reason hunted; and no sooner had,
Past reason hated, as a swallow'd bait,
On purpose laid to make the taker mad:
Mad in pursuit, and in possession so;
Had, having, and in quest to have, extreme,
A bliss in proof, and prov'd, a very woe;
Before, a joy propos'd, behind, a dream:
　　All this the world well knows; yet none knows well
　　To shun the heaven that leads men to this hell.

—WILLIAM SHAKESPEARE

A Waste of Shame

A Short Novel

Chapter 1

We stood in the woods, Jim had the shotgun, my back was turned to him, and I was sure he was going to take aim and fire. I bet he did take aim, too, and if it hadn't been for Don, his sidekick witnessing it all, he'd have pulled the trigger.

That probably flashed before Jim's eyes. He puts the bullet through my head, says something like, "Brought him down with one shot," watches my body spasm for a few moments as blood pours out of my skull, and then says to Don, "You say anything and I'll blow your head off, too," or something like that.

At least that's what I thought he might do after I said I was going back to the farmhouse. Why the heck did I go into the woods with them in the first place? What did I think I was going to miss? Jim, the braggart, in his mackinaw and duck boots, showing us how accurate a shot he was? Or Don, the dullard, in his flannel and loafers of all things, analyzing our every action?

"I don't think Kevin could fire it anyway," Jim said, referring to me. "There's nothing in his shoulders. This shotgun's got too much kick."

"That's OK," I said. "I don't want to shoot it."

"Why wouldn't you want to shoot it?" Don asked.

"I don't like guns," I said.

"Are you philosophically opposed to firearms?" Don asked.

"No. I don't like 'em, that's all."

However, I really wanted to pull the trigger. I'd done air pistols and bb guns as a boy, but never fired a shotgun big enough to bring down a deer. I'd held one but never felt its full power, was at the point of taking the gun from Jim, but then hated him; was not going to let him teach me anything, be superior to me at anything.

Maybe he hated me, too. I think I could see it on his face as he held the shotgun, not looking into my eyes, but *at* me or *through* me, taking all the expression off his thin face which contrasted with his pudgy body. Lately, he'd looked drawn. He was definitely losing weight. Probably the stress of what he was doing, so that the prominent brow bones and cheek bones protruded while his eyeballs sunk back into their cavities, very much like a skull. His hair was a mousy brown, or more like a dog brown or a rat brown. Yes, a rat brown.

Don, the skunk, the city boy, he was all gung-ho about going into the woods and shooting squirrel or a twig off a branch of a log.

"This is boring," I said. "I'm going back to the farmhouse. I might even go back home."

"Go," Jim said. "I mean, what the fuck did you come out here for?"

That "f" word stung me. I hate that word. He knew it, too. The prevalence of that word today is evidence of the corruption of our language, which is evidence of the corruption of our society, and evidence of his corruption.

"Maybe I'll go back and chat with Debra," I said. And I meant that to sting, too.

Yeah, I'll talk to Debra, I said to myself as I pushed through the woods, bare branches and pine needles flicking across my face. I'll tell her the truth. I'll tell her what a lying piece of crap she has for a boyfriend. I'll tell her not to marry that a-hole. I'll tell her not to give birth to his child.

But it was a long walk back to the farmhouse where Jim and Debra lived, across a creek, down a log trail—on which I walked the wrong way for about a hundred yards —through another stretch of bushwhacking before I saw the A-shaped red barn, the rusty farm equipment, and the freaking mud hole that surrounded everything; the fenced-in field with the two milk cows, the small pad for the pony, the chickens scratching in the front yard, beside the road, right in freaking front of me; and the house, the rotten house, covered with peeling reddish brown paint, the color of dried blood.

The screen door squeaked and slammed behind me. The entryway stunk of onions and cow crap. I walked into the house. Debra was chopping mushrooms with Jim's long-bladed cook's knife.

"Well?" she asked. Debra didn't look six months pregnant. But I didn't know what six-months pregnant should look like. She wasn't showing at all, or, if she was, she was covering it with a loose-fitting blouse. She did glow a little bit, I suppose. Her cheeks looked ruddy. She was not a beautiful gal, but attractive, cute, with short, curly brown hair, a freckled complexion and wide-set eyes, like a horse. And wide hips, too, for giving birth.

"Well, what?"

"They right behind you?"

"No!"

"Didn't you kill a bird or something?"

"No. I didn't kill a bird," I said. "That Don's intolerable."

"Yeah, he's a pain in the behind."

"He's boring. He analyzes everything."

"I don't understand what Jim sees in that guy. He's odd."

"Probably because he worships Jim," I said. "Jim can do no wrong. Jim is some superman, an American folk hero, a Paul Bunyan."

"I think you're exaggerating." Debra went back to slicing mushrooms, knuckles on the blade, like Jim taught her. Like he taught me. "Were they right behind you?"

"No. I left them back there in the woods. Don wanted to see Jim shoot the wings off a fly or some bull crap like that."

"I'm making omelets. Are you staying?"

"I don't know." Why would I want to stay? To take some perverse delight in this ironic situation, watching this tragedy unfold like some spectator in a theater unable to shout out, "Hey, you there, guess what?" Why couldn't I shout out? What was stopping me?

"Why aren't you gonna to stay?"

"I don't know."

"What are you gonna do, go home?"

"I guess."

"And do what?"

"I don't know."

So I sat at the kitchen table reading the humorous anecdotes in the *Reader's Digest* while Debra sliced cheese. What I should have done was to have skulked under the kitchen window and slipped into the car Mom let me borrow, and taken off without going into the house or even saying goodbye to Debra, and maybe to have never returned. But while I was thinking this and watching Debra whip eggs, the screen door squeaked and in they came, not 15 minutes behind me, Jim carrying the shotgun.

"Is that gun unloaded?" Debra asked.

Jim didn't answer, but his squinting eyes brushed across my face, catching my eyes. He could tell I hadn't told Debra anything. I wouldn't have had time anyway. But, God, if I wanted to tell her Jim was cheating on her, I could, couldn't I?

"Did you shoot that fly off the twig of the log at 50 paces?" I asked.

"We were trying to hit tin cans," Don said, giving a serious answer to a rhetorical question.

"You sure didn't," Jim said to me.

"I didn't have anything to prove."

"We didn't go out there to prove anything," Jim said. "We went out to shoot a gun."

"We didn't hear any shots," I said. "At least I didn't. Did you, Deb?"

"No."

"Eh. Why waste good deer slugs at 20 cents a piece?" Jim asked.

"What?" I asked, incredulously. Inside, I was saying, I know why the freaking hell Jim cut short this escapade. Funny how poorly he lied. How come she didn't see it? How come I didn't see it before?

We ate our omelets. Jim let us know they weren't what he'd classify as perfect, meaning Debra had flipped them—and that's verboten—but that didn't stop him from wolfing his down like a farm dog.

I thought the avocado was a great touch and told Debra so. Even Don gave Debra a compliment, and Jim finally had to back off of this purely academic discussion on how to make an omelet, though Don had to quote Lenin who said that in order to make an omelet you have to break a few eggs. I said, yeah, what else would you expect a mass murderer to say, which ended that discussion.

When I scraped the last forkful of egg off my plate, I was all set to move on, to exit stage right, to get in Mom's car and go home. And I would have, if the beer hadn't come out.

Then began our beer discussion. What was the best beer? Jim and I both agreed that when our local brewery bought out a small Canadian brewery, including its prestigious name and its entire remaining stock, for maybe two months we'd never tasted finer beer, until they began to insert the new beer into the old bottles. It then became a beer best vomited. Don said that he had a similar good experience with Canadian beer in his home state of Michigan. Debra had fond memories of a Pennsylvania beer, which triggered memories of her alcoholic father who quit drinking on his thirtieth birthday. On the one-year anniversary of that event, he celebrated with champagne and didn't stop again until he died.

Then we matched drunk stories. My best was visiting my cousin in Buffalo, going to a bar called the Emergency Room where a shoot-out ensued, then getting smashed and passing out in a puddle of my own vomit. Jim's was walking on a bridge railing over a local creek and falling, luckily, into deep water, barely missing being impaled on a post. Don's was getting blotto on Kailua the night before an 8 a.m. college chemistry exam, taking it still drunk, and still getting a B+. Debra said she never remembered losing control like that.

"You better stay here tonight," Jim said to me about eight hours later.

"I can't," I said. "Mom has to have her car by 7:30 in the morning. She has to go to work."

"Can't you sleep here for a few hours and then go home?" Debra asked.

"If I fall asleep now, I won't wake up until noon. Mom has to have her car and that's the end of it."

"Don't you have an internal clock?" Don asked. "All of us possess one."

Jim and Debra followed me as far as the back entryway and, from the opened screen door, watched me stumble to the car, pile in, turn on the ignition, repeatedly rev up the engine, throw it in drive, and whip onto the highway. Then I turned up Braxton Road, deciding to drive the back roads, the way any smart drunk would go.

I passed cow pastures on either side and then a big old farmhouse and weather-worn barn on the right. The road curves around the bottom end of a forested ridge. On the left nestles a small house and across the road a barn and a small pasture hewn out of the woods. Then comes a series of wooded S-curves with a sharp turn to the right. Very sharp.

Somehow the steering wheel wouldn't turn fast enough and the wheels couldn't negotiate the curve. Suddenly, the car was driving at a 45-degree angle in a gully until, as I remember, the car stopped.

I exited the driver's side as if I were emerging from a submarine hatch. The cool air hit me like a sobering slap. And there I stood, in the dark and quiet, on a country road, drunk at two three a.m., two three miles from the farmhouse, three four miles from home, with Mom's car in a ditch.

I decided to run, down the wooded S-curves, around the ridge, past the barn, back to Jim and Debra's farmhouse, lights already out, running down the road to the very man I imagined was going to shoot me in the woods, now seeking his help, like a battered, chained-up cur wagging his tail when the master brings out the slop.

It took a few minutes for the lights to flick on after I pounded on the door. Jim answered. Half his face was dark pink and lined with creases as if he'd fallen asleep on corduroy.

"You idiot," Jim said. But he dressed and put on his mackinaw, and we hopped into the cab of his pickup, hardly saying anything. He took those curves faster than I but negotiated them successfully.

"It's right around this corner," I said. Between the moonlight and the headlights, we got a good look at the absurd position in which my car had stopped. Jim chained the front of the bumper to the back of his truck and instructed me on how to turn the wheel. I got back in, again submarine-style, and he used his truck to lurch the car out of the ditch and upright. He then walked around the vehicle, looked at the mud and the rusted body parts scraped out. Jim gave a hearty laugh as he pulled out a large clump of swamp grass by the driver side door.

"I hope it starts," I said. "Mom's got to be to work by 7:30." How many more times was I going to say that? I turned the key and it started.

"You're lucky," Jim said through the opened car window. "You're like a cat always landing with his feet on the ground."

"Must be my guardian angel," I said.

"More like dumb luck," he said. "You gonna chance driving that thing home?"

"You don't think it'll make it?"

"Probably."

"Besides, Mom has to have her car."

"You better take it to a car wash first."

"At three in the morning?"

"Better get the hose out."

"I don't care. As long as it runs." There was this long, wee-hours-of-the-morning silence. "Listen, Jim. Thanks a lot."

"I've got to get back to bed."

"OK. See you at work." And that was it. I got the car home, no problem. Should've washed it though, because Mom said that I wouldn't be allowed to drive it for a month. That laying down the law lasted three days.

Chapter 2

I wish Jim had never told me about Pam. But he did, in August at the end of our shift at the Blue Anchor Restaurant.

After breaking down the grill and the fryers and turning off the kitchen lights that night, Jim and I sat at the bar drinking our usual imported Canadian beer. Tony, our boss, said something like, "Good job you guys. We did 245 tonight."

"That many?" Jim asked.

"Yep," Tony answered.

"We ran out of lobster," Jim said. "And I shouldn't have served that last one. I think it was too small."

"Not a single complaint," Tony said, and he returned to the counter where he totaled his receipts.

Most of the waitresses had counted their tips and left, but that night Brenda sat at the bar sipping vodka and orange juice, ring on every finger, pinky in the air.

"So?" she asked.

"So?" Jim said, imitating the inflection of her voice.

"So, is it true?"

"Is what true?"

"You and Pam."

"What about me and Pam?"

"You two were seen together in your truck in downtown Bartlett."

"Like you could call the four corners downtown," I said, trying to get into the conversation.

"By who?" Jim asked.

"Tony."

I looked at Tony. He looked up from the receipts toward us, then quickly looked away.

"Big deal," Jim said.

"Then you admit it?" Brenda asked.

"Admit what?"

The significance of their conversation didn't register. Brenda liked to joke, and even if Tony did see Jim and Pam together, so what? They work together. We all do.

Brenda left. Tony finished tallying the receipts. Princess, Tony's wife, came in. This was Tony's cue to say, "All right you guys, that's it," which was our cue to quickly swill our drafts.

I hopped into the cab of Jim's pickup and opened the window all the way, leaned my head out, and listened to the gravel under the truck tires. The light over the front entrance flicked out.

As we pulled out of the driveway, I looked across the road at Livingston Lake. The lights from the summer cottages necklaced the shore. The cool air felt good after a hot evening cooking in the kitchen.

"You're probably wondering what Brenda was talking about," Jim said, as we turned onto Town Line Road. I was looking at a dilapidated house partially hidden behind an oak tree.

"What do you mean?"

"About Pam."

"You mean about you and Pam in downtown Bartlett?"

"Yeah."

Then silence. I was savoring the ride, the cool air, the trees flickering by, that feeling you get from having done a full day's work and done it well.

"You're not curious?" he asked.

"A little, sure." We were passing Bartlett Gas Station.

"I'm seeing her."

"Uh huh."

At that point, I was thinking about the time Jim's truck had broken down, and we had to walk to the station to get a tow.

"We're seeing each other. You know. I'm bedding her."

I looked at him. He kept turning his head toward me and then back toward the road. He grinned, probably hoping to see me grin too and say something like, "You devil you," or "Get it while you can." But I said, "What do you mean?"

"I'm screwing her."

"What about Debra?"

"I'm screwing her, too."

"That's not what I mean."

"I know what you mean."

"No, you don't," I said. "When did this happen?"

"A couple of months ago."

"A couple of months ago?"

"Yeah, a couple of months ago," Jim said, looking straight ahead at the road. "One night a bunch of us took a swim after work. Pam wanted me to take her home."

"But she's still in high school."

"Yeah, but she just turned 18."

I thought, yep, if I had a car maybe I could get a girl, too. Not having any wheels was a drag. Then I rolled up the window because the air was getting cold.

"But what about Debra?" I asked again. "She's pregnant."

"I know."

I persisted. "You're going to be a father."

"I know."

"Don't you love Debra anymore?"

He banged his hand on the steering wheel and I shut up. He probably expected this reaction or he would have told me sooner.

That last mile we were quiet. When he stopped in front of my house I said, fishing, "You going straight home?"

"What do you think, we see each other every night?"

"I don't know."

"Listen, Kevin, I've been struggling with this. I know it's not right. I keep telling her we're going to have to stop, but she's all over me. She's really a wonder woman, you know."

This time I grinned back.

Chapter 3

Pam shut her car door and stood waiting for us to pull into the parking lot of the Blue Anchor at the start of the evening shift. She mock smiled, hand waving close to her face as if she hadn't seen us in a year, looking more at Jim than at me. Jim and I stayed in the truck as she approached my side. I put my hand through the opened window and hooked my finger through one of the belt loops on her pants.

"Jim, Occy's at it again." She gave my hand a weak slap.

"Stop calling me that."

"Then stop it."

"Yeah, stop that," Jim said.

"I can't help it," I said, grinning. She grinned, too. Then I pulled back into the cab while she poked her head in. Why not go around to the other side and make kissy face with Jim, I wondered.

She had a pretty head, too—fluffy brunette hair feathered around her face, sparkling green eyes, and two slightly crooked front teeth.

"Occy, did you get into trouble with your mommy this morning?"

I didn't play coy and say, "What do you mean?" or play dumb and say, "Who told you that?" Of course she knew that I drove mom's car into a ditch. That was probably their pillow talk that afternoon, if the back of a truck seat could be called a pillow.

"No, I didn't get in trouble."

"You want to come to the cabin with us tonight?" Pam asked me. Her eyes became like nickels, and she spoke to me as she might speak, lollipop in hand, to a three-year old.

"What cabin?"

"My parent's cabin."

"And do what?"

"Hang out with us."

"And do what? Watch you two slobber all over each other? And what am I going to do, whittle twigs?"

"My friend Tanya's going to come along."

"Oh, yeah?"

"But I've warned her about your eight arms, Occy."

"You make me sound like a pervert."

"You gonna come?"

"Yeah, come on," Jim said. "We'll pick up a case."

"What choice do I have? I have to ride with you."

"I'll drop you home first if you want."

"What's she look like?"

"Cute," Pam said. "But naive. She's perfect for you."

"What do you mean naive? You think I'm naive?"

Pam winked at Jim.

During the evening shift I thought about the cabin. At one point, Pam came back into the kitchen, and she and Jim tried to grab each other with metal tongs. I watched, the perennial outsider.

Waitress Brenda stuck her head through the kitchen window. "All right, you two. Stop horsing around." Then she checked the plates. "There's no lemon on this one."

Jim pointed his tongs at me, playful smirk still stuck on his face. Then the smirk vanished. "You gotta pay attention," Jim said. I was in charge of all garnishes and fish platters, and he, as head chef, was in charge of me.

"Yeah, Occy, get it together," Pam added, pinching my arm with a tong.

"Occy?" Brenda said.

"Yeah," Pam said. "He's all arms, like an octopus." Then she swirled her arms around her chest and did her impression of an octopus.

I was too embarrassed to look at Brenda as I put a lemon wedge on the fish platter. Brenda made a last check, then did a balancing act with her plates.

Tony's head replaced Brenda's in the window. "Pam? There are a couple of dessert orders here. Let's go."

Jim and I watched her exit.

Chapter 4

Mom yelled "Kevin" up the stairs. She used a voice like shimmering tin, a tone she honed trying to rouse my brother and me for school. She hadn't practiced the instrument for some time, but she hadn't lost her mastery of it.

"Kevin," she yelled again, this time taking a few thumps up the stairs.

"What?" I yelled with the same pitch and volume.

"It's noon, for Christ's sake. Debra's here."

I heard their voices as I came down the stairs, Debra's nasal and flat, Mom's sing-songy and grating.

"You're a bear when you wake up," Mom said.

"Who wants to be woke up by a fog horn?"

"I'll remember that the next time you want to borrow my car," she said.

Debra stood in the kitchen in a pair of strap-on sandals and a halter top, pregnant belly slightly protruding. Mom wouldn't approve of that outfit, I was sure, and would bring it up later, as if I could do something about it. I wasn't sure I approved of it either.

Debra didn't interfere, but let us get the back and forth out of our systems. Then Mom went to her corner, that well-worn depression on the couch accommodating her oversized frame across from the 36-inch TV broadcasting a game show which she didn't turn off or turn down.

"I was at the Laundromat and thought you might want to go to Auntie's Kitchen for lunch," Debra said to me.

"Lunch?"

"Breakfast. Something."

"I guess."

"You don't have to."

"No, it's all right."

"You sure?"

"Let me drag a comb through my hair."

When I came out of the bathroom, Debra and Mom, sitting on opposite sides of the couch, looked like two large knickknacks from different eras, both with brown curly hair, both sucking nicotine.

"Phew. When are you gals going to give up those cancer sticks?"

"When you and your brother get off my back, maybe I'll do it."

"When are you going to give them up?" Debra asked me.

"I don't smoke."

"What were you doing the other night?"

"Smoking, but I only smoke when I drink."

"Uh huh."

"Good one, Debra," Mom said.

"Okay, Okay. Let's get out of here."

A person has to drive a couple of miles down a country road to get anywhere in Livingston County—one long country road to a gas station, another to a bar, and still another to the next village, which is what we did. Debra drove fast though, and we pulled into the driveway of Auntie's Kitchen probably before the engine got warm.

A short square woman limped to the table and dropped off two grease-stained menus.

I had trouble looking Debra in the eye. Instead, I looked at her breasts. She didn't have much up top to begin with, and the halter top flattened them to her chest. She didn't seem as pretty as when we first met, either. Tiny creases fanned out around her eyes.

She smiled; I didn't. I couldn't. I had the fixed image from the night before of Jim and Pam as they climbed, one right after another, into the loft at the cabin, his hands on her behind, followed almost immediately by their soft groaning as I sat by the flickering logs, sparks flying upwards, trying to make conversation with that dimwit Tanya. How long had I sat in front of the fire watching the birch log turn into ash, the beetle ramble to the topmost gnarl, then fall, shriveling into the fire?

My eyes scanned Debra's face, hers mine, and then finally she caught my eyes and held them steady.

"What are you thinking about?" she asked.

"My mind's a blank," I lied. "I have a bit of a hangover," which was half-true.

"How many times have you guys gone out drinking this week? Four?"

"Not me."

"No?"

Then I thought, God, did I blow Jim's cover?

"Well, maybe you're not drinking too much, but Jim is."

"I don't think so."

"Every time he comes back from work, he's drunk."

"After work everyone ends up at the bar."

"Not at the restaurant where I work."

"Maybe you should change restaurants."

"Why, so I can become a drunk too?"

"I'm not a drunk."

The waitress hobbled back. It looked like every step she took hurt.

"What happened to you?" Debra asked her.

"Old age."

Debra tried not to laugh but couldn't contain herself. The waitress put her arms on her hips, looked Deb up and down, then said: "You think that's funny? You'll know what I'm talking about soon enough."

"I wasn't making fun of you," Debra said.

"I know what you were trying to do."

Deb's face blotched red.

When the waitress left, Debra said, "Jeesh, I thought she was trying to be funny. Didn't you?"

"I don't know."

"I didn't mean to offend her."

"Don't worry, she looks like a tough old bird."

"I hope I'm not still waitressing at her age."

Suddenly, glass shattered in the kitchen.

"Good one," one of the patrons at the counter shouted. Then we heard yelling. "You stupid bitch."

"You want I should retire?" It was our waitress.

"Will you please, you arthritic cow?"

"Shove it up your ass."

Then the conversation died.

"I'm getting sick of Livingston County," Debra said.

"What do you mean?"

"It's nothing but a bunch of lowlifes and rednecks."

"Which one am I?"

"Please."

"Which one is Jim?"

"Now that's a good question." She took a swig of water. "I've been thinking about going back to Pennsylvania."

"Back to Pennsylvania?"

"Yeah, back home."

"Why?"

She craned her neck forward, looked at me slit-eyed, and said, "I don't feel that Jim wants to be a father."

"Why?"

"Since he found out I'm pregnant, he's drunk all the time."

"It was like this before."

"I don't think so."

"I do. We've been drinking buddies a long time."

"And you don't help matters any."

"What do I have to do with it?"

"Once in a while can't you say, 'Enough?'"

"I'm not forcing him to drink." I realized I was speaking too loudly, so I brought the volume down to a near whisper. The waitress hobbled toward us again, carrying two cups of soup with one hand and a basket of bread in the other. Her hand shook as she slid the saucer on the table, spilling a significant amount of my soup into it, then shoving the cups in front of us.

"She stinks," I said after she left. "I hope you're a better waitress than she is." I poured the spilled soup back into the cup before sipping a spoonful.

"God, you're noisy," Debra said.

"Yech. Campbell's."

"No, it's not. Look, there's chicken skin in mine. It's homemade."

"Well, maybe half. These peas are from a can."

"What do you expect?"

"I can imagine what Jim would have to say about this," I said.

"Like Jim's the be-all and end-all of food."

"He knows his stuff."

"He thinks he does."

"What?"

"Forget it."

She was halfway through the soup when she resumed the conversation. "I can see I won't get a straight answer out of you anyway."

"About what?"

"I've been wanting to talk to you for days."

"About what?"

She sighed. "About Jim."

"What about Jim?"

"Do you think he wants to be a father?"

"Oh. I don't know."

"You should know."

"Why should I know?"

Our waitress clunked down our main courses. Debra had a BLT. I'd ordered the chicken salad sandwich.

"What a mistake," I said.

"What?"

"Ordering chicken salad. It's drenched in mayo." I touched it with the tip of my tongue. "No, this isn't mayo. It's *Miracle Whip*. Yech. This is crap. Damn it. I'm not eating this freaking stuff. I should have asked first."

"Scrape some of it off," Debra said.

"I don't eat *Miracle Whip*."

"Well, if you were in Pennsylvania, that's all you could get."

"That's why I'm not in Pennsylvania."

"To hell with your sandwich anyway. This is a little more important."

"What's more important?"

"What I'm going to do."

"Go back to Pennsylvania?"

"No."

"Then what?"

"Have an abortion."

"An *abortion*?"

"God, you're dramatic," Debra said.

"Mom says that, too."

Debra ate her sandwich. I looked at the food and listened to the clatter of dishes.

"Well?" Debra asked.

"Well, what?"

"What do you think?"

"I don't know."

"Aren't you gonna eat your sandwich?"

"I'm gonna take it home and wash off the *Miracle Whip*."

"You're funny."

"I think you should think more about it before you do anything," I said after a long gap of silence.

"The decision gets easier by the minute."

"What do you mean?"

"Something's wrong. I don't know what it is. He's too young or something. I don't know."

"He'll grow into the idea."

"This is not an idea," she said, pointing to her belly.

I shook my head. "I can't speak for Jim."

"But what do you think?"

"I don't know."

"You're a big help."

Chapter 5

I rested my head on the kitchen table, using my forearms as a pillow. I must've heaved several sighs, but who could hear over Mom's soap opera? Sappy strings tried to direct her to feel trepidation over some immanent doom. Did so-and-so leave what's-his-name? Did whose-its murder whatya-call-him? But the commercial break happened and Mom said, "Don't you have anything better to do?"

"No."

"Why don't you go outside and blow some stink off you?"

"No." I let my lips touch the metal table top. "I don't want to."

"What? I can't understand a word you're saying."

"I said, no."

The soap opera came back on for the last segment, the climax that would have to hold Mom for the next 23 hours.

"Listen," she said, finally turning off the set. "You're going to have to get out of the kitchen."

I rested my head sideways on one of my arms. "Why?"

"Because I've got work to do?"

"What work?"

"I'm going to can some dilly beans."

"Right now?"

"As soon as I do up the dishes."

She turned on the faucet and gave three good squeezes of detergent into the sink. The last sounded like a fart. Tiny bubbles floated upward.

"How can you stand hot water like that?" I asked, watching the steam rise from the sink.

"When you've scrubbed as many floors and washed as much laundry, and did as many dishes as I have, you'll know."

"I don't think that's gonna happen."

"When are you going to get out of here and leave me to get my work done?"

"I don't know. I don't really have anything to do."

"Why don't you call Jim?"

"Nope."

"Why didn't you stick around with Debra? That was a quick lunch."

"She had stuff to do."

Mom started scrubbing the dishes. She kept the water running and rinsed each dish after washing it. I have a different method of doing dishes without filling the sink with water. I soap up the pad, scrub all the dishes, and then rinse them all at once. Forget about making a freaking production out of washing dishes.

"Debra's thinking about leaving Jim and going back home to Pennsylvania," I said.

"What?"

"Yep."

"When did she tell you that?"

"About an hour ago."

"Christ," Mom said. Mom was one of those types that, when she swore, she never used the "f" word or anything vulgar; instead, she took the Lord's name in vain. "Why?"

"That freakin' Jim," I said. "He's a real a-hole."

"I thought you guys were best friends."

"I thought we were too."

"Weren't you two out drinking last night?"

"Yeah, that sonofabitch."

"Let's tone it down," Mom said.

"Tone what down?"

"Your language."

"What should I say? He's screwing somebody else?"

"Huh?"

Mom turned off the spigot. This one was worth a sit-down with her son. It hadn't happened often: after the death of a grade school friend as a result of an accidental shot gun blast, the time I broke into and trashed a vacant house, Dad's death—stuff like that warranted Mom breaking from her usual TV patterns or busy work.

She actually wore a startled expression, not the angry one I usually saw. Her hair was beginning to get awfully gray, too, I noticed.

"What do you mean he's screwing somebody else?"

"About two months ago I found out that he was running with this girl we both work with."

"She from around here?"

"No."

"Would I know her?

"No."

"How did you find out?"

"That's a good question. Everybody else seemed to know what was going on. I think Jim only told me because he couldn't keep it a secret anymore."

"When did Debra find out?"

"She doesn't know."

"Oh, Jesus."

About that time the back door opened. We knew because the pull of the air from the entryway caused the kitchen door to rattle. Then my brother Timmy barged in.

"Don't you know how to knock?" Mom asked.

Timmy was dressed, as usual, in his favorite pair of jeans, threadbare holes in both knees. He wore his red-brown hair at eyelash length, which he constantly had to flick out of his eyes. He was attempting to grow a beard. He didn't bother to say anything, snuffled and spit whatever he found in his sinuses into the sink.

"God," Mom said. "Can't you do that outside?"

Timmy began to root around the refrigerator.

"What are you looking for?" Mom asked.

No reply. He finally found some lunch meat, opened a package of bread on the counter, and dug out four slices from the middle of the loaf.

"What's the matter with those first couple of slices?" I asked.

No response. "Close up that bread," Mom said.

Again, nothing. And he was out the door, back to his lair above the garage.

"When are you going make him pay some rent?" I asked.

"I didn't make you pay rent at age 17, did I?"

"But at least I did something around here."

"Let's not start."

Timmy must have heard me because, as he walked past the kitchen window, he knocked, we looked up, and he flipped me an obscene gesture.

"You two," Mom said.

"Damn him," I said.

"I wish you two got along."

"We would if he did something around here."

"Listen, if you're going to start, I don't want to hear it. Find something to do."

"I don't know what to do."

"Clean your room. Rake the yard."

"No. That's not what I mean."

"What do you mean?"

"I don't know what to do about Debra."

"What about Debra?"

I let out an exasperated grunt. I banged on the table, rattling a fork.

"Don't be so dramatic."

"I'm not being dramatic. That freakin' bastard."

"Hey, hey. I won't have that talk in my house."

"I don't freakin' care. What am I supposed to do?"

"About what?"

"Damn it. Forget it."

"How can I help you if you don't tell me?"

"You can't help me."

"What do you mean, I can't help you? You think your mother hasn't learned a thing or two in 46 years?"

"It's not that."

"Then what is it?"

"Listen. We're at Auntie's Kitchen. Deb says she doesn't think Jim wants to be a father and she wants to know what I think. I wanted to say to Deb, 'He's freakin' cheating on you'; and I'm thinking how to tell her the truth and what her reaction will be; and, as I'm about to tell her, she blurts out that she's thinking about having an abortion."

"Oh, Jesus."

"Now tell me, you really think you can help me?"

"Well, I'll tell you right now, whether she has an abortion or not, whether she stays with Jim or not, don't tell her a goddamn thing."

"What?"

"Don't say anything," Mom said, more like a command than a request. "It's none of your goddamn business."

"But it is my business."

"How?"

"Because I know, that's how."

"I'm telling you, stay out of it."

"But I don't want to see Deb hurt."

"You're not responsible for Debra."

"But what kind of friend would I be?"

"Look, he could come after you," Mom said, and again, for a brief moment, another emotion other than anger broke through. "Didn't Jim's father once land in jail for assault?"

"So?"

"OK. Do what you want."

"I can't tell her anyway. I don't want to be responsible if she has an abortion."

"Good. Then go your separate ways."

"But I work with him," I said. "Jim's my boss, remember?"

That stopped her. What really would happen if I told Debra? Would I have to quit my job and hang around the house, interfering with her soap operas?

"Why don't you wash the car and then go put some gas in it?"

"When's the last time he put gas in it?"

"Your brother?"

"Yeah. He uses it as much as I do."

"Christ."

"You want to use it again, don't you?"

"Yep."

"Then get out of here and leave me alone."

Chapter 6

Debra glowed. She effervesced. She was obnoxious. And Jim too. He had an ear-to-ear grin and exhibited these wise and smiling eyes.

"Hey buddy," Jim said, patting me on the back. Debra kissed me on the cheek. That was a new one, very sophisticated, very grown-up. Quite a build-up for a trip to the college bars in Hadleyburg to get tanked on *Blatz* or three-for-five dollar *Old Vienna*s.

We laughed. We joked. Jim let out those "ha ha ha's" that hung over the top of the din, which, I distinctly remember, caused the din to diminish because self-conscious college students don't often hear or produce that kind of laughter. Debra snorted. I did what I rarely do— allowed my teeth to show when I smiled.

But why shouldn't we make merry? Debra and Jim had set a wedding date.

"Beautiful," I said. "Congratulations." What a relief, I thought. I won't have to be in the middle anymore. "You guys were made for each other," I continued. "You practically look like brother and sister."

They looked at each other. We clicked glasses. They rubbed noses and gave each other beery kisses. Jim patted Debra's pregnant belly.

"When are you getting married?" I asked.

"Two weeks from Saturday," Debra said.

"That's quick."

I looked at Jim, who met my eyes for an instant, then looked away.

"Where?"

"Back home," Debra said.

"In Warren?"

"Yep. Then we're gonna spend the night in Niagara Falls."

"That's a lot of driving," I said.

I grabbed Debra's pack of cigarettes and picked one out. "You mind?"

"Go ahead," Debra said. "You've smoked half my pack already."

"Sorry." I lit it, and took a deep drag. As I let out the smoke, I asked, "What's Tony gonna do on Saturday with you gone?"

"I was thinking you could take my place," Jim said.

"That's not what we talked about," Debra said.

"I told you Tony won't go for having us both out on Saturday."

"Go for what?"

"Debra thinks you should be my best man," he said, not looking at me. "But I don't see how."

"Best man? What does that mean? What's a best man supposed to do?"

"Stand there like a idiot," Jim said, and laughed.

"He does not," Debra said, giving his arm a good swat.

"Then what?"

"He toasts the bride and the groom at the reception," Debra said.

"In front of everybody?"

"Yeah."

"Anything else?"

"I don't know. What else? Jim?" she asked, turning toward him. But before he could think to answer, she said, "Technically, he serves as a witness."

"A witness?"

"Yeah," Jim said. "You get to witness a man's last moment of freedom." As he said it, he put his wrists together as if shackled. We all laughed.

We stayed until the bars closed and then had to decide who had drunk the least. I knew I couldn't drive. Then Jim declined. Debra took the wheel.

We drove up the hill to the top of Hadleyburg-Pomfret Road and turned onto West Lake Road. Debra took it slow, careful. We encountered patches of fog. Then something struck us as funny—Debra let out an unladylike belch or something—and we began to laugh. Next Jim told Debra to watch out for the turtle in the road, and Debra slowed down to a crawl because she didn't like to hurt animals; but it turned out to be a hubcap, and we laughed some more. Then, suddenly, blinking lights appeared behind us. We sat up straight, thinking cops had spotted us, but the car honked as it passed us because we drove too slow, and then we laughed some more. Debra sped up and into a thick patch of fog. The road turned, I think. Maybe we hit a patch of black ice. I don't know. The car spun one way.

"Turn the wheel," Jim instructed.

The car swung the opposite direction. "Take your foot off the brake."

We bumped into a field, a fence appeared, the car jolted, and then it stopped. Debra gave it more gas but we didn't move.

"Take your foot off the gas," Jim ordered.

"Way to go, Deb," I said.

"You think you could do any better?"

I followed Jim out of the car, taking two beers from a case behind the front seat, handing one to him. Debra piled out, cigarette dangling from her lips as she slammed the door.

"It's cold out here," she said.

"Look at that," he directed. "We're right on top of a downed tree. How the hell did you do that?" Jim walked around the side. "The front wheels aren't even touching the ground." As he cracked his fist on the hood, he said, "Fuck."

The conversation stopped while we swigged our beers. Debra blew out a cloud of smoke, and Jim and I might as well have been smoking because our breath hung in the air.

"Why don't we walk," I said. "We're about two miles from my house and I could drive you to the farm in Mom's car."

"I think we should try to push it out," Jim said.

"Oh, brother," Debra said.

"Get back in the car and drive," he said to Debra. "You push from the driver's side, and I'll push from the passenger's side," he said to me.

I positioned myself.

"OK, give it some gas."

The front tires spun.

"Now push."

"I can't get a footing. My shoe's slipping."

"Hold up, Deb" he said. "Kevin, put your foot on that log."

I did.

"Now put your weight against the front."

"All right."

"Now watch what I do."

I repositioned myself.

"Okay, Deb."

"Okay, what?"

"Give it some more gas."

She did.

"Now push."

"I am."

"Push harder."

"I'm trying."

"Rock it back and forth a little."

"I can't," I said, taking my hands off the truck and backing off. "Forget it." If it hadn't been for the headlights, I might have missed Jim's quick, mean glance.

We began to walk, at first along the main highway, later detouring along the old railroad track bed, a shortcut that stretched straight along the side of Maplewood Lake.

The county had torn up the tracks a decade earlier, but the gravel track bed remained for most of its length. Sumacs and berry bushes had encroached some sections, but mostly it was passable.

"You have an extra cigarette?" I asked Debra.

"Why don't you buy your own?"

I shut up and listened to the ambient noise, footsteps on gravel, bushes whacking our bodies. A small animal scurried in the brush.

"What time is it?" Debra asked.

I started to say something but decided to let Jim answer, but he didn't.

"What time is it?"

We arrived at the swampy outer edge of Maplewood Lake.

"Can one of you guys answer my question?"

"How should I know?" Jim asked.

"It's a simple question," Debra said.

"It's gotta be at least 3:30," I said.

"I don't think it's that late," Jim said.

We passed a stretch of swamp that took us very close to the lake's edge, allowing us to see the lake's expansive dark surface for the first time.

"I'd say we have about three quarters of a mile to go," I proffered.

"You wearing a pedometer?" Jim asked.

Then we passed a string of lakefront cottages, all dark, except the last, which had on an outside light. The rest had been vacated for the season. On the far side of the last cottage, Jim spotted a row boat.

"Hold up a second," he said, jumping a gully.

"Why?" I asked. "Let's keep going. We're almost home."

"It's cold," Debra said.

"Look, there's oars underneath."

"We can't take someone else's boat," I said.

"Why not?"

"It doesn't belong to us."

"We can return it tomorrow."

"Let's do it," Debra said.

"It's even gonna be colder on the lake, you know."

"Stop jabbering and help me turn this boat over," Jim directed.

Jim and I tipped over the heavy wooden row boat, then shoved it into the water.

"How am I gonna get in there?" Debra asked.

"I'll hold it steady while you step in," Jim said.

"I'm afraid I'll fall in."

"I'll put it alongside the dock," Jim explained. "How about that?"

Debra climbed in front while Jim and I held the boat steady, then I climbed in the back. Jim sat in the middle, facing my back. He shoved us off. With two strokes, drawing each oar in opposite directions, he had the boat turned around and headed toward the village dock in Maplewood.

We listened to the plash of the oars and the creaking of the oarlocks as Jim stroked.

"We should go fishing before the lake freezes," I said to Jim, but he didn't answer.

"Remember that bass I caught last May?"

"We both caught it, you idiot," Jim said.

"It was my pole."

"What happened?" Debra asked.

"His line got tangled and the reel fell off," Jim said. "I'm the one who pulled the fish in."

"A four pound, 18-1/2 inch smallmouth bass. Remember?"

Jim didn't respond.

"Don't you remember?"

"I don't think you'll ever let me forget."

"Why not?" Debra asked.

"Because Jim bet me who could guess the length of the fish and I said 18-1/2 inches and Jim was way off, and when we measured it, it was exactly 18-1/2 inches from the head to the crook of the tail."

"All right," Jim said. "Let's drop it."

"But then Jim said, 'Was your guess 18-1/2 inches to the crook or to the tip of the tail,' like that half-inch was going to make a freakin' difference."

"All right already."

I didn't realize the boat leaked until I heard water splash when I moved my shoe. "Are we taking on water?" I asked.

"I hope not," Debra said.

"Feel between the slats," I said to Jim.

"It is a little bit," Jim said.

"I don't feel anything," Debra insisted.

"It's above the slats back here," I said. "Listen." I splashed the water with my shoe.

"Let me see," Jim said, leaning toward me. I moved aside to let him reach the floor, but when I shifted, the boat rocked. "And stop with the jerky movements."

"Now it's really coming in," I said.

"It's probably our combined weight."

Jim leaned back and began rowing harder.

"I have to put my foot up or my feet are going to get soaked."

"It can't be coming in that fast," Jim said.

"Oh my God, there's water up here," Debra said. Her sharp voice carried across the water.

"Keep it down," Jim said to her. "Maybe the drain plug is missing. I didn't check."

"Drain plug? Why would there be a drain plug? You mean they deliberately put a hole in the bottom of a row boat?"

"It would be in the back, not the bottom."

"Why?"

"If there's a big rain or if your boat sinks, then you want to have an easy way to drain it."

"Are we sinking?" Debra asked.

"Of course not," Jim said with authority.

"I'm telling you right now, this water is really coming in."

"Well feel around, find the hole, and plug it up."

"This water is freezing," I said.

"You find it?"

"I can only put my hand in for a few seconds."

"Goddamn it. Plug it up or I'm gonna have to come back and do it."

"I feel where the water's streaming in and there's some sort of a wooden cork or something. I'm gonna try to push it. Goddammit."

"What happened?" Debra asked.

Jim stopped talking and rowed like a sonofabitch.

We were probably a hundred feet from the end of the village dock when I began to think we might not make it. As we reached the end of the dock, the lake breached the back end of the boat and it began to sink. Debra screamed. Perhaps we traveled two more yards, and then it sank in three feet of water.

"You fuckin' idiot," Jim said to me.

"It was your idea to take the boat," I said.

"Why didn't you leave it the fuck alone?"

"I didn't do anything."

"Then what happened?"

"We made it, didn't we?"

"It's cold," Debra said, her teeth chattering.

"I wonder what Mom's going to say when we wake her up?"

Chapter 7

Timmy's Halloween party started with a parade of high school guys, six packs in hand, piling out of rusted pick-up trucks and climbing the stairs over the garage into a smoky room where loud music blasted through tall free-standing speakers.

I don't know how he finagled the presence of Diane, cheerleader, since my brother floated with the vocational trade students and not that heady jock circle. But she was there, along with three of her not-quite-as-cute girlfriends, one of whom brought Juanita, a plain and plump foreign exchange student from Mexico.

Timmy had purchased a keg and strung black-and-orange crepe paper and balloons, tacking them to his ceiling with great care. He'd also vacuumed, and he must have powdered the shag carpet with baking soda or talcum because the place didn't smell like the usual musty beer-soaked dish rag.

After I'd settled into a bean-bag chair and hit the three-beer threshold—meaning once I'd reached three I couldn't stop—Jim arrived. Don, his sidekick, followed immediately behind him, wearing, of all things, creased pants.

"What are you doing here?" I shouted to Jim, ignoring Don, except to note he'd purchased a new pair of glasses with thick exactly rectangular lenses.

"Your mother said you were up here."

"What?"

"Your mother," Jim yelled, pointing in the direction of Mom's house, then pointing to me.

For a few minutes one of my brother's friends, who'd brought the latest record from a metallic-sounding Southern rock band, cranked up the volume. Several of them joined in the refrain.

"My brother's throwing a Halloween party."

"Looks like high school."

"Hard to pass up a keg."

"Huh?"

"Want a beer?"

"Sure."

I walked over to the keg where my brother and a couple of his cronies stood guard.

"You mind if they have a beer?" I asked my brother.

Timmy glanced at them, glanced at me, shrugged, then went back to sizing up Diane and the girls huddled together in a giggling clique. I expertly filled three plastic cups to capacity, minimum foam, as if I had a certificate in bartending.

We picked a spot away from the two free-standing speakers, but near enough to the keg, which sat in a round metal tub surrounded by chunks of ice. The beer went down smooth. Timmy—or whoever it was who bought the beer for my underage brother—had paid a few extra dollars and purchased Canadian.

Timmy came over to me and said, "You better fork over some money for all the beer you guys are drinking."

"He speaks," I said to Jim and Don, as if a lightning bolt struck, juiced Frankenstein, and gave us proof positive that the brain transplant worked.

"I'm not kidding," he said.

"Okay, we will."

I looked at Jim and Don, thinking they might divvy up or maybe at least pretend to reach in their pockets but each looked at something else. Then Jim took a long swig.

"I'll give you some money later," I said. But Timmy turned his back on me and walked toward Diane and the girls.

"Let's go over to Harry's Tavern and have a few," Jim said.

"Why not hang out here?"

"Is this the only style of music your brother likes?" Don asked.

"I don't know what kind of music he likes," I said. "Take a look through his records," which Don did for the next half hour, sitting on the floor, records between his legs, reading record covers, taking records out of their jackets, and examining the quality of the vinyl.

"Where's Debra tonight?" I asked Jim.

"I don't want to talk about that bitch."

"Huh?"

"When I told her I was going to go out to have a drink, she blew a gasket. Said I was a drunk."

I was starting to get tanked. Jim may have had a few before he came.

"Hey, you gotta cigarette?" I asked one of my brother's beer buddies. He pulled a pack out of his denim jacket and jerked it, causing exactly one filtered cigarette to stick out. He grinned. He was either proud of his feat or proud that he smoked.

"I think you're getting hooked on those things," Jim said. "You've got a monkey on your back."

I looked over both my shoulders. "No, I don't."

"When you've got a monkey on your back you're not free." He took a long swig, then got up and poured out another beer.

"Look at this," Don said. "You think your brother would mind if I played it?"

Others had changed records; no one seemed at the helm, so I said, "Wait'll this song finishes." The song Don played was kind of rock and roll and kind of twangy at the same time, a tune with a sappy story.

A couple of the guys groaned when it started. Someone said, "What is this shit?" But they let it play almost to the end before the needle scratched across the vinyl and another replaced it on the turntable—a song with screeching, inaudible lyrics.

I felt a tap on my arm. "Don't let him do that again," my brother said to me.

Jim's eyes had become slits by the time the subject of Debra came up again.

"I thought you guys had worked everything out."

Jim sat there trying to think and talk at the same time. Something tried to bubble to the surface. One of my brother's recessed lights shone directly on Jim's face, making it seem as if he were being interrogated. However, he didn't move out of the light.

"The plans have been made, right?" I asked him.

"I don't want to marry that bitch."

I shook my head a couple of times like a deer flicking off flies.

"Everything was perfect the other night."

"The car goes off the road, and then we nearly drown."

"You two were all lovey-dovey. You put your ear to Deb's belly."

"That kid. Stupid," he said, banging his fist on his thigh, then swilling another long drought. "This is good beer," he said.

"We're going to have to come up with a few dollars for the beer."

"All I have is a twenty."

I spotted Juanita, standing within earshot.

"*Hola*," I said, summoning my knowledge of two years of high school Spanish.

Juanita smiled, making her cheeks even plumper.

"Hello," she said, moving closer.

"*Como estas?*"

"You idiot," Jim said to me.

"Good, and you?" She asked.

"*Muy bien. Yo estudio español hace . . .* Jim, do you remember how to say it makes so and so many years that I studied Spanish?"

"*Dos*, you idiot." Jim had been in one of my classes.

"Please," she said. "In English."

"*Pero, yo . . .* "

"Please, no Spanish."

There must have been drama in the way Juanita held up her hand and shook her head "no" that made Diane walk over and grab her arm.

"These two bothering you?"

"No."

"Come over here," Diane said, after she eyeballed us. A couple of old lechers, she probably thought, though she did smile at me. I figured she knew I was Timmy's brother. As Diane turned, her thick sandy-blond, shoulder-length hair fanned out.

"Cunts," Jim said.

"Why do you have to talk like that?"

"And Deb's the biggest cunt of them all."

This last thought hung in the air like cigarette smoke. Maybe he assumed I was pondering his profundity, but what I was pondering was why the hell he wanted to get married and why the hell he didn't tell Debra about Pam."

"What are you going to do?" I asked.

He shrugged his shoulders and took another long swig, finishing the contents of his plastic cup. This time he didn't immediately get up to refill it—probably too tanked to exert the energy. He waited for me to finish mine then had me do it.

"You gonna get married or what?"

"How can I get married to someone I don't love?"

"You don't love her?"

"I'm in love with Pam."

"I thought you weren't seeing her anymore?"

Jim looked to the side, probably some expression he learned as a boy after his father asked him if he knew who broke the neighbor's front window when he'd known full well he'd done it himself.

"You're not, right?" I asked.

"Look at this Beatles album," Don said, interrupting us. "This is pristine. There's not a scratch on it."

"Fuck the album," Jim said. Don took the cue and buzzed off. I poured us two more beers.

"Pam's the best fuck I've ever had," Jim said when I returned.

"I don't want to hear about it."

"She's incredible. You know what she did Thursday?"

"I thought you weren't seeing her anymore."

"She was a virgin you know."

"You're right back to where you were a couple of weeks ago?"

"There's nothing like popping a cherry."

Jim assumed the position of Rodin's *Thinker*, but sitting Indian style, his chin held up by one arm.

"I don't know what I'm gonna do," he said.

"Why don't you tell Debra you're seeing Pam and get it over with?"

Jim let out an audible breath of air, put his head down, and ran his hands through his hair.

"Well?" I said.

"Well?" he said, imitating my voice.

"Why don't you just tell Deb?"

"Why don't I just tell Deb?"

"Are you making fun of me?"

He looked up and eyed me with a mean, penetrating stare.

"I'm just asking a question," I said.

"If I knew what to do I wouldn't be sitting here drunk."

"If you told her, she could have an abortion."

"She's not having an abortion."

"No?"

"We talked about that already."

"What if she knew about Pam?"

He must have misread the tone of my voice, because he started to rise. "You better not tell her about Pam." And then I think I misread his actions because I thought he was going to punch me.

"I gotta take a piss," he said. He stood for a moment, lost his balance, tried to catch himself, thumped the floor hard enough to make the room shake, and then fell onto one of my brother's friends who helped him stand upright. The kid said, "You all right?"

"Yeah. Where's the bathroom?"

"Downstairs in the garage," I said.

He steadied himself and slowly descended the stairs, a hand holding up each wall.

A few songs later Don came over to me and said, "Where's Jim?"

"The sonofabitch probably passed out."

"Maybe we better check on him."

"He's old enough to take care of himself."

"He looked pretty drunk."

Don descended the stairs. I bummed another smoke and inhaled very deeply, causing a long portion of the cigarette to glow. I looked up at a balloon, then at the end of my cigarette, pulled myself up, took a furtive glance toward my brother in conversation across the room, and popped the damned thing. A couple of guys looked over. My brother, from across the room, said, "Hey." Then I, too, made my exit.

I didn't see Jim in the toilet or in the garage. As I walked outside, the screen door snapped back, echoing in the alley between the houses. It wasn't enough that the neighbors had to endure the house vibrating or the cars revving up their engines, they also had to put up with that freaking door.

I could see Jim's red pick-up truck but where the hell was he? As I approached the truck, I heard the gut heave of a man puking, walked around the truck and saw Jim on his knees behind a blue van, his arms on the bumper, letting go the contents of his stomach. He groaned. Don stood aside looking on.

"You all right?" I asked.

"Uh."

"I didn't think he had that much to drink," I said more to myself than to Don.

"He was drinking shots at Harry's Tavern before we came here," Don said.

Jim let go again and then groaned some more.

I stood there thinking maybe Jim deserved to heave out his innards. Maybe if a person poked around the alcohol soup he'd deposited, they could find his heart or his brains.

"You gonna drive him home?"

"Yeah," Don said.

"You got your keys?" I asked Jim

Jim reached into his pockets, a hand still on the bumper. He vomited one more time.

"Oh, God," he said.

I grabbed him by his arm to drag him up. "Come on," I said but, as he stood, Rodney, one of my brother's friends, slipped out of the shadows.

"What the fuck did you do to my van?" he asked, looking straight at me, obviously judging me by the company I keep. I didn't respond. "I said what the fuck did you do?"

"Nothing," I said, but better that I hadn't because, with his pointed boot, he aimed a kick at my crotch. I flinched backward, barely escaping serious injury.

"Puke on your own fucking car," he said, then got into his van, revved up the motor and spun out, flinging stones.

"Asshole," I said.

Not until Jim and Don had situated themselves in the cab did Don realize that Jim's truck had a standard shift, and he didn't know how to drive it. He nearly backed into a tree before I realized that I had given him opposite directions on how to shift gears, but he finally figured it out and lurched off slowly.

After they left, I walked along the garage approaching the snapping door to my brother's lair, sure that I would continue past it and into the house, run upstairs and fall into bed. But as I neared it, three of my brother's friends emerged. I could have walked around them, but I stopped and held open the door for them. One of them said, "Hey, take it easy." Then I made a choice. A door had opened and I entered.

As I reached the landing at the top of the stairs, Diane was trying to poke her arm through the sleeve of her varsity cheerleader jacket marked with the school letters. Her girl friends flanked her sides while Juanita stood behind in the shadows.

"You leaving?" I asked.

"Yeah," Diane said.

"Too bad," I said.

The ends of her mouth curled into a smile and her nose crinkled.

"You're cute," she said.

"You are too," I said, and suddenly our faces came within breathing distance, which is probably the closest I've ever gotten to a cheerleader. Her breath smelled beery.

She put her lips to my ear, "You're cuter than your brother." Our cheeks brushed together. Her hair smelled smoky clean.

"Thanks."

"God, I think I've had too much to drink," she said, snapping me back to reality.

Suddenly my brother appeared at my side, then pushed in front of me, nearly stepping on my toe.

"Need help getting to your car?" Timmy asked.

"No," she said. "We're all right."

We watched them descend, but, before they reached the last stair, Timmy turned toward me and said "You fucker" loud enough for my ears only.

"What do you mean?"

"Why don't you throw your own party?"

I responded by going to the keg and filling up another plastic cup.

"Gimme some money for the beer," Timmy said.

"I said I would."

"Then hand it over."

"I don't have it on me."

"Then that's the last beer."

The girls were gone; only Timmy's core group of cronies remained. They started a contest to see who could shout the loudest. Then one guy shoved another who pushed him back. He then tried to unbalance another. In moments, a group wrestling match ensued with this tiny mob shifting to the left, and falling en masse, some on the bed and some on the floor, knocking objects off the nightstand. They laughed and shouted. Someone said, "Get off me, you fucker."

I bummed another smoke from the cigarette guy.

"I should have bought a pack," I said.

"No problem. Take a couple."

"One's enough."

Then I saw the balloons again—my cigarette and a large balloon. Pop.

"What's that, a gun?" someone asked.

"Cut it out," Timmy said. The mob quieted.

I honed in on another one. Pop. And that was it. My brother extricated himself from the throng and from some deep part of himself shouted "Goddamn you" as he started toward me.

I bolted down the stairs. He must've taken the steps two, three at a time, because in a moment he was behind me, pushing my back. I ran faster, snapping the door, but he didn't relent.

"You goddamn sonofabitch. I'm going to kill you."

I imitated the sound of his voice, no words, only the tone, taunting him. As I ran into the back entryway of Mom's house, I shoved the door in his face. I couldn't quite close it. He pushed with all his might. He didn't have my weight or my strength, but that night, maybe because I was drunk or because of some burst of his adrenaline or some deeper motivation on his part, I could feel myself losing the war. I let go and made a dash for the heavier kitchen door. I slammed it to give myself a minute before running into the kitchen.

"You bastard," Timmy yelled.

We'd fought before, we'd gotten into shouting matches or tussles, but something in his voice made me take him seriously.

The back porch light shone through the kitchen windows, illuminating the stainless steel sink and the enamel kitchen table.

"Knock it off," I said. I ran around the table. "Cut it out."

"I'm going to kill you."

"You're going to wake Mom."

"I don't care."

We circled the table again. And again.

"Damn it. Knock it off."

"No," he yelled, and as he uttered the word he grabbed the table and flung it upward. As it spun, it shattered the ceiling globe.

At that moment, Mom jumped out of bed and thumped through the dark house.

"Goddamn you two. What do you goddamn kids think you're doing? Get the goddamn hell to bed." With each word came the accompanying rhythmic thump of her footfalls, like the telling of a primitive poem. Then, almost like a plaintive refrain, came a very long and loud "Oh, Jesus" as she entered the kitchen.

Timmy bolted. I turned on the light. Mom had made her way to the bathroom indicated by a trail of blood which began from a sharp shard protruding from the bottom of what a moment before had been a drinking glass. It must have set on the table when Timmy threw it.

I found the broom in the corner and began sweeping. Broken glass had reached the hallway by the bathroom, and, as I approached the door, Mom said, "Goddamn you two."

"I didn't do anything."

"What do you mean, you didn't do anything?"

"I didn't fling the table in the air. I didn't break the glass."

"Get me a clean towel."

I hesitated to go in.

"I said, get me a goddamn towel."

I entered. She sat on the tub's edge, her back to me. When she spoke, her words reverberated inside the enamel hollow of the basin. "I wish your father were alive," she said.

I'd never seen that much blood.

"Listen, Timmy's the one that started chasing me. He's the one that threw the table in the air."

"Is that what happened?"

"Yeah, he threw the kitchen table in the air and broke the ceiling globe."

"What did you do to him?"

"Nothing."

"You must've done something."

"I didn't do anything."

"Then why would he chase you?"

"Because he was drunk, because I flirted with the girl he's interested in, because I popped one of his freakin' balloons."

"I don't know," Mom said. "I can't stop the bleeding."

"What do you mean, you can't stop the bleeding?"

"What did I step on?"

"The bottom of a glass I think."

"Get me the hydrogen peroxide." I did. She poured it on her foot without flinching. "I can't understand you two."

"I told you I didn't do anything."

"You act like two-year-olds or a couple of drunks. You certainly don't act like brothers." She turned around. "Give me another towel."

"How are brothers supposed to act?"

"Don't start with me." She threw a second blood-soaked towel near the first and wrapped her foot with the third. "I don't know if this is going to stop bleeding."

I went back to sweeping the glass in the kitchen. I upturned the table. As I picked pieces of glass off the stove top, Mom hobbled through the living room and back into bed.

"I'll tell you this much right now," she said from the other room, "you're not getting the car for a while."

"How am I going to get to work on Thurdays and Sundays?"

"You should have thought of that before."

I was too tired to argue. I slumped at the kitchen table with my head in my hands.

"How about turning the light off and getting to bed?"

"In a minute."

"Now."

"In a minute."

A minute passed.

"Oh Jesus," Mom said with alarm.

"What?"

Nothing.

"What is it?"

"I can't stop the bleeding. You're going to have to drive me to the emergency room."

"I thought you said I couldn't have the car."

"Don't start with me."

So I drove Mom to the emergency room where she received seven stitches on the arch of her foot, three pints of blood, and a prescription for iron pills.

Chapter 8

As I tied my apron, waitress Brenda walked up behind me in the kitchen entranceway and put her cold hands on my neck.

"What did you do to your mother?" she asked.

"What?"

I turned. She wore massive, dangling half-moon earrings.

"We heard your mother lost a lot of blood and was rushed to the hospital the other night."

"Where'd you hear that?"

"Tony mentioned it."

"Well, I don't know where he heard that because he doesn't know what the hell he's talking about."

"Okay. Okay," she said, fleeing to the pantry.

I stood for a moment before entering the kitchen and thought, how could anyone know about Mom? I didn't tell Jim. I wouldn't. Mom, Timmy and I had all agreed that the episode shouldn't leave the house.

As I entered the kitchen, Jim whipped eggs for the fried catfish special while Pam stood behind him clutching his arms, pressed against his back, pretending to see what he was doing.

She would look over his shoulder or around his chest; he would pivot and furtively keep the stainless steel bowl from her eyes. Pam giggled. Jim laughed. Give me the bowl, I thought, then I can puke in it.

"Hey, Occy."

"What's up, buddy?"

Buddy? Now I'm his buddy? "Nothing."

"Your mother Okay?" Jim asked.

"Whadaya mean?"

"Is," Pam said slowly, "your mother—that is the woman who raised you—Okay—meaning is she all right? Duh."

"My mother's fine, thank you," I said.

"That's not what we heard," Pam said.

I walked over to my station and began pulling down the ingredients from the shelf to make the Blue Anchor's famous fish fry-beer batter. They watched me as two might watch a gladiator girding his loins—bug-eyed, tongues hanging out, probably breathless. I finally deigned to notice the two hams.

"Well?" Pam asked.

"Well, what?"

"What happened to your mother?"

"Nothing."

"That's not what we heard," Pam said.

"What did you hear?"

"That your mother went to the emergency room."

How the hell could they know that? "You guys are nuts."

"We'll get it out of him," Jim said, and they dropped the subject. They went back to their goo-gooing and coo-cooing while I exacted the right amount of paprika, salt, beer, and the secret ingredient that made our fish taste distinct.

The rush hit early. All of Livingston County must have decided to eat at the Blue Anchor that night, and they mostly ordered deep-fried seafood. I had haddock lined up in perfect rows covering most every square inch of surface grease in four fryers. Both French fry baskets sizzled non-stop for the better part of five hours. At one point, Jim had to mix an extra bowl of beer batter for me and bring another box of haddock out of the walk-in.

I marveled at myself, at my performance that night: spinning on the balls of my feet, pulling down plates, garnishing each one, doing a one-eighty to get the fish and fries and again to fill the plates, checking new orders, and again pivoting to put down half a dozen filets into the bubbling oil. That night I may have hit the high point of my fry-cook career, given the high volume of orders, the smoothness with which they went out, the fact that not one mistake had been made, that we served them in a timely manner, and that at the end of the rush I'd felt a deep sense of accomplishment—even before Tony came back to compliment me.

"Good job, Kevin," Tony said, patting my shoulder.

"Yeah," Brenda said, following Tony into the cramped space behind the counter. As she said it, she adjusted the chain link belt around her ultra-thin waist.

"We're in record fish fry territory tonight," Tony said.

"You think so?" Jim said.

"It sure felt like it," I said.

"I've seen us busier," Jim said.

God, couldn't Jim give a little credit where credit was due? Couldn't he say, "Good job," or, "Well done?" Instead, he has to diminish perhaps my greatest night as a fry cook; my smooth, seamless, flawless cooking display.

Pam appeared, her apron covered with a chocolate stain. She'd probably spilled hot fudge down her front while making a sundae.

"470 dinners tonight," Tony said to Pam.

"Cool."

"And for a change you stayed at your station."

"Where else would I be?"

"Jim, where else would she be?" Tony asked.

Jim pretended he didn't know, did a kind of Stan Laurel imitation, exaggerating his eyeball movement, pursing his lips while pretending to whistle, twiddling his thumbs. Then Pam stepped into Jim's side of the kitchen, wrapped her arms around his shoulders, and they posed for Tony, Brenda and me with big, dumb grins on their faces.

"I meant to ask you," Tony said, turning to me. "How's your mother?"

"I . . . " I started to say.

Brenda interrupted. "You got it wrong about Kevin's mother."

"Oh?" Tony said looking at me, his forehead wrinkled with four, deep equidistant horizontal lines. "Princess thought she saw your mother at Hadleysberg Hospital yesterday when she was visiting her father."

"She must have seen someone else."

"Your mother's name is Shirley, right?"

"Yeah."

"And she had a blood transfusion, right?"

I hesitated. "Yeah."

"You lie," Brenda said.

"No, I don't."

"You're lying now."

"No, I'm not."

"What do you call it?"

"I don't want to talk about it."

"Why not?"

"It's personal."

"Tell us."

"No. I don't want to."

"What's the big deal, Occy?" Pam asked. "I mean, your mother went to the hospital. So what?"

"I don't want to talk about it," I said.

"Brenda, don't you have tables to check?" Tony asked her.

"Yeah."

"Well, check them."

"Damn." Brenda pirouetted, taking exaggeratedly large, high steps toward the dining room.

"And what about you?" Tony said to Pam. "Don't you have a dessert order to fill?"

Pam leaned over the counter and poked her head through the kitchen window where she could glimpse that no dessert orders had been clipped to the pantry window. "No," she said.

"What about clean up?"

"I'm almost done."

Tony shrugged, then turned to me. "I wanted to talk to you about next Saturday."

"I'm not going to be here."

"That's what I wanted to talk to you about."

"I'm going to be best man at Jim's wedding."

"Well," Pam said. "This is where I leave you guys. I don't want to hear anything about Jim's wedding." As she left, she put her fingers in her ears and started singing to drown out the conversation. Jim pretended to boot her in the rear, an action she missed. She also didn't hear us laugh.

"I don't think it's going to be possible for you to go," Tony said, resuming the conversation, looking more at Jim than at me.

"I can't miss Jim's wedding. How can I miss his wedding? Jim, come on, tell him."

"You see the way it was tonight," Tony said.

"But this is Friday," I reminded him. "Saturday's different."

"I want you to be the lead cook on Saturday."

"You could do it, too," Jim said.

"What? Don't you want me to be your best man?"

Jim didn't answer.

"I thought you had everything worked out," I said to Tony.

"I thought so, too, but I have to do what I have to do."

"All right. If that's the way it has to be. Wait. Jim is my ride on Saturday. How am I going to get here?"

"How about your mother's car?" Jim proffered.

"You know she uses it on Saturday."

"If I have to, Princess or I will pick you up," Tony said, while massaging his forehead.

"Christ," I said. "I guess you guys have it all worked out." I looked at Jim, and he looked at me with a droopy, woeful countenance, probably reflecting mine.

"Good," Tony said. "That's settled. I've gotta get back to the bar." He patted my shoulder as he exited.

"How can I miss your wedding?" I asked Jim.

"It's no big deal."

"It is a big deal."

"Deb'll show you the pictures."

"Wait'll Deb finds out."

"She already knows."

"Deb knows I'm not gonna be there?"

"Yeah."

"Why didn't you tell me?"

"I don't know."

Jim started to scrape the grill. "What's the big deal with your mother anyway? Did she hurt herself the night of the party?"

"You'd already gone; you were smashed."

"What happened?"

I told him. It was the first time I'd told the story, and my face must have flushed from the saintly way I portrayed my behavior and the devilish way I portrayed my brother's.

"Don't tell anybody," I said to Jim. "We'd rather it not be general knowledge."

"OK. We better start breaking down the kitchen."

"Order up," Brenda said.

"They're still coming in?" I asked.

"It's an eight top," Brenda said. "But only one ordered dinner. The rest are having drinks and dessert."

"Did you place the dessert order yet?" Jim asked.

"No."

"Gimme that desert order." Jim grabbed it and raced to the pantry window. He spent the next 20 minutes assisting Pam while I cleaned my half of the kitchen to a sparkling shine.

Chapter 9

On the afternoon of Jim's wedding, I floated into the kitchen and saw Tony at Jim's station, wearing an apron and cutting and weighing portions of prime rib, Saturday's big seller. Tony's mouth hung open the way a kid looks trying to balance himself walking the top of a fence. He exhibited steely concentration as he tossed a slab of beef on the scale. He took his eyes off the meat, looked at me for a moment, same expression, then back at the meat.

"That the special tonight?" I asked.

"Yep."

I put on my apron. At least wearing mine didn't cover a gut like Tony's.

"You going to stand there or are you going to get busy?" Tony asked.

"What needs to be done on Jim's side?"

"It's all prepped."

"My side too?"

"Nope."

"Oh well. Thanks for doing that side," I said. "I appreciate it."

He ignored me. I continued to stand there, watching him slice through another rib. "That's an awful big piece of meat," I said.

"You think so?"

He put it on the scale: 18 ounces, six ounces too much.

"You're going to make some customer very happy."

He looked at me and shrugged his shoulders as if to say, "I'm the owner and if I want to serve 18 ounces of beef, I will."

"Don't you have something to do?" he asked.

"You're doing it."

"Whaddya mean?"

"I thought I was head cook tonight." He stuck the blade back in the meat and began another cut.

"I think I'm going to do it," he said, not looking at me.

"You said I was going to do it."

"I'm not sure you can handle it."

"What do you mean?"

"If we have a rush like we did last week, I don't see how you'll be able to do it."

"We never have a rush on Saturday like the rushes on Friday when everyone comes in for the fish fry."

"You never know," he said, gripping the knife.

"I do know. I've worked here for two years."

"Listen, I have a business to run, and I want to make sure it's run right."

"You mean by giving people 18 ounces of prime rib?"

"I don't want to argue about it."

I shrugged my shoulders and opened the walk-in cooler. I pulled the door closed, giving it a good slam. I stood there looking at the filthy walk-in floor and smelling

74

rotting tomatoes and rancid fish. I put my nose to the box of haddock. "Phew." The door flew open.

"Don't be slamming the door," Tony said as he reached for a box of parsley.

"You think this fish is any good?" I asked him.

"Sure."

"Smell it," I said. He did.

"No problem."

"It's slimy."

He touched it.

"Wash it off," he said.

"You sure?"

"Yep."

He let the door gently close, which meant it didn't latch, didn't seal tight. I gave it a good shove to show how he should shut it. He should freaking know that the reason the fish is spoiled is that no one knows how to freaking close the freaking refrigerator door.

That bastard Jim, I thought. Or maybe Tony was the bastard. Why did Jim say I was going to be head cook? The whole idea of my coming into work was to do Jim's job and allow him to go to the wedding. If Tony was going to do it, I could have gone to the wedding. My freaking best friend was getting married, and I had to freaking come in to cook spoiled fish.

Rinsing the slime off the haddock, running it under the cold water, rubbing it with salt and rinsing it again, calmed me. No way we could save the whole box. It wouldn't last another day. But who couldn't tell a fresh piece of fish from an old one, even deep fried? Or maybe Tony figured right; who out here in the sticks would know the difference?

"Occy!"

I turned around. Pam stood a couple of feet back, arms on her hips. "Why aren't you on the grill?"

Before I could answer, she turned to Tony and with the same tone of voice, those same wide-open, unblinking, puppy dog eyes, said: "Tony, how come you're cooking?"

"Don't you have work to do?"

Suddenly, Pam pressed behind me and whispered in my ear, "God help the customers if he's cooking tonight."

"I know," I said, twisting my neck back to see the crinkles in her face as she smiled. "What time is it now?" I asked.

"4:20."

"Jim is probably freakin' nervous he's about ready to walk up the aisle."

She recoiled. "I don't want to talk about it."

"But I bet he is."

"You think so?"

The mirth left her face, replaced by a look I'd never seen before, not on her, not on anyone. No eighteen-year-old should look that troubled, that wise.

"Don't you have work to do?" Tony said to Pam again. Pam exited without another word.

The night passed quickly, smoothly; the business steady. No rushes at all; one order then another, which didn't confound Tony. But he put out his plates without artistry, without an eye to the plate's beauty. If beef juice dribbled on the side of the plate, he didn't wipe it off, and more than one went out without the steak knife, except for Brenda's plates. She made them look pretty. That night she wore green eye shadow.

"Damn it, Tony," Brenda said at one point. "These plates look ugly."

"Not as ugly as you," he said, flicking a parsley sprig with his tongs a la Jim, but without Jim's accuracy.

Pam stayed out of the kitchen, preferring to remain inside the pantry like a denned animal. I noticed her face —her unsmiling profile—at the pantry window from time to time. "What a boring night," I said to Tony, if he might be listening, or to anybody else.

"If you think this job's boring, maybe you should find another one," he said, which shut me up again.

I began to break down my side, turning off two of the fryers and opening the valves to strain the grease into a bucket. Tony's wife Princess strode into the kitchen. "How much longer?" she asked him.

"As long as it takes."

"What do you mean?"

"I don't know, thirty to forty-five minutes."

Princess brushed her bright copper-colored bangs out of her eyes. Tony put the finishing touches on the last order of the night, serving the last piece of prime rib—a gristled end cut—and a shrimp scampi. He hadn't yet started scraping the grill or wiping the side board. Jim would have had half his station scraped and scrubbed. "I've got all this clean up to do," Tony said.

"Can't he do it?" she asked, referring to me.

Tony didn't answer but did ring the bell five times in a row to let Brenda know her order was ready. Then he said, extra loud, "Order up" and rang the bell five times more.

"Did you forget the Andersons?" Princess asked.

"The Andersons?"

"Yes. We're meeting them for drinks at the Rusty Shield."

Tony grunted. "Oh, yeah."

Princess turned to me. "Could you clean up tonight?"

I heaved a sigh, the usual response when a woman tells me what do, though she didn't exactly tell me.

Tony said, "That's not right to ask him that, Prin."

"Why not?"

"You see that, Tony?" I asked. "If you would have let me be head chef tonight, this wouldn't have been a problem."

"Who would have cleaned up your side?" Tony asked.

"I haven't had an order on my side for a half an hour. You would have been half done by now."

"We've been over that already," Tony said.

"Well, if you didn't need me tonight you should have let me go to Jim's wedding. I was supposed to be his best man."

"Really?" Princess asked.

"Yeah."

"Are you sure?"

"Yeah."

"Tony," Princess said. "Do you think Jim wanted Kevin to be his best man?"

Tony ignored her.

"Ignore me," Princess said. "That's what you usually do."

"Drop it."

"No."

"Like I said before, thirty to forty-five minutes, but the more you keep badgering me, the longer it's gonna take."

"If Jim wanted you to be his best man, why did he practically beg Tony to make you work tonight?" Princess asked.

"I said, drop it," Tony barked, raising his voice. And then to Brenda, "Order up, damn it." He rang the bell again.

"What do you mean?" I asked.

"He pleaded with Tony to find a way to have you stay here tonight."

"Then why did he ask me to be his best man?"

"Jesus, sweetheart, I don't know. But, trust me, I could have done your job tonight."

"Really?"

"Who do you think was the fry cook when Tony and I started the business?"

Brenda finally picked up the plates. "It's about time," he said to her as she raced to the dining room.

"That's the last time I tell you anything," Tony said to Princess.

"You think you can keep anything from me, darling?"

"Fuck it," Tony said, throwing his wash rag on the stainless steel. "Listen, can you clean up here for me?"

"I guess so," I answered. "It's not right, though."

"You'll get paid for it."

Tony whispered to Princess as they walked out of the kitchen, loud enough for me to hear, "You've got a big mouth, Prin."

As I polished the stainless steel countertop, Pam turned off the lights in the pantry.

She untied her apron and headed in the opposite direction of the kitchen. "Hey," I yelled. "Aren't you going to say goodnight?"

She turned around and said, "Goodnight, Occy."

"You wanna do something later?"

"No."

"Why not?"

"I wanna go home."

"You wanna go for a beer or a walk down by the lake?"

"No."

"Why not?"

"I don't feel like it." I edged closer to her, and we toned down our voices.

"What would you like to do?"

"Go home, I told you."

"And do what?"

"Think."

"About what?"

"You know what."

"Or should I say about whom?"

"That's it. I'm going."

"Why?"

"I don't want to talk about it."

"Why not? It's a fact. He's married. You can't change it now."

"I know."

"Why did you have to remind me about it before?"

I didn't answer.

"Why not shoot me? It'd be less painful."

She started to turn. I touched her shoulder.

"Occy," she said, looking at my hand. I put it back in my pocket.

"You sure you don't want to do something?"

Pam shook her head. "Do you think he's doing the right thing?"

"What do you mean, the right thing?"

"Getting married."

"Yeah. Why not?"

"Isn't she a bitch?"

"No. She's Okay."

"That's not what Jim says."

"He's also going to be a father."

"She trapped him."

"It takes two," I said.

That's when she broke down and cried. Snot streamed out of her nostrils. I wanted to put my arms around her, but I didn't dare. I wanted to say something to her, but I didn't know what. Suddenly I heard Brenda's voice. "What did you do to her?"

"What do you mean?"

"What did he do to you?" Brenda asked Pam.

"Nothing."

"Come on, honey. Let's go have a drink," Brenda said, putting her arm around her shoulder.

"Okay," she said. "You have a tissue?"

Chapter 10

Jim called a couple of days after he got back from his wedding. The bastard's truck broke down, and he hoped I could pick him up on Thursday to go to work.

"Who is it?" I asked Mom after she'd lumbered across the living room to pick up the receiver. She tried never to let a phone ring more than twice, something she'd learned as a telephone operator before the advent of the rotary phone, which hadn't hit the sticks of our state until the early '60s.

"Jim," she said.

I shook my head, no.

"You get over here and answer the phone."

"No."

"Jim, he'll be right with you."

With her hand securely over the mouthpiece she said, "You get over here right now, buddy, or I'll tell him you don't want to talk to him."

"Fuck."

"What did you say to me?"

"Forget it."

I let out a full steam of air as I approached the phone.

"Stop being so dramatic." Then she uncovered the receiver.

"Hello?"

"Hey. What's up?"

"Hanging out."

"How did it go the other night?"

"I wasn't head cook."

"No?"

"Tony didn't trust I could do it."

"Huh?"

"That means I could have gone to your wedding. Princess could have handled the fryers. It wasn't that busy anyway."

"I guess he needed you."

You freaking liar, I thought. Why didn't want me at his wedding? To stop me from talking to Debra? Because I wasn't his best friend? That's some of what I thought, but what I said was, "I guess."

"So," he said.

"So," I said.

"So, you wanna go drinkin'?"

Sure, I thought. Go drinking with a freaking liar. "Where?"

"We'd have to go to Harry's, unless we can use your mother's car."

"Can't we use your truck?" As I said it, Mom's head jerked left, as her concentration switched from her TV show to my telephone conversation.

"It's broke down. I had to take it to the garage."

"Broke down?" I asked. "What happened?"

Mom took that as her cue to bolt off the couch, thump across the floor, and wag her finger in my face. "You're not taking my goddamn car tonight." She still wore an Ace bandage on the foot cut by the shard of glass.

"You must have ears the size of radar dishes," I said. "Hold on a minute." I covered the receiver. "Why not?"

"Because I'm taking it."

"Where?"

"What difference does it make where? It's my car."

"Damn it."

"I thought you didn't want to see him."

"Keep your voice down," I said, waving her off. Then I spoke to Jim again. "If you can get here, we can go to Harry's." Harry's was the local tavern located a half mile from Maplewood if you took East Lake Road but less than a quarter if you walked the short cut through the woods.

"I guess Deb can drop me off in her car and pick me up after she finishes work." Then he added, "What's the matter, your Mom won't let you take her car?"

"Well, it's her car."

"Okay. Harry's is as good a place as any. But tomorrow you can pick me up and take me to work."

"I can't believe you," Mom said when I hung up the phone.

"What do you mean?"

"An hour ago you said you didn't want to speak with him and now you're going out drinking with him."

"So?"

Mom palmed her forehead in a melodramatic gesture, then shook her head. "Like I said, I can't believe you."

I puttered around the kitchen for fifteen, twenty minutes, and then began to straighten the telephone books and the junk behind the telephone.

"Why is all this junk here?" I asked. "Couldn't you get rid of some of this crap?"

"It's my house and if I want to have junk up to the ceiling, I will."

"You do now anyway. I mean, look at this TV tray. You opened it a couple of months ago, and now it's one more place to pile your soap opera magazines and all this other crap."

"You should talk."

"What do you mean?"

"Go upstairs and take a look at that pigsty."

"Where do you think I learned it from?"

"I think you'd better get the hell out of here before I kick you out of here."

"I'm going."

"When?"

Mom heaved one of her usual sighs which corresponded to the exhalation of a large drag off an unfiltered cigarette. Then she coughed.

"What's the matter with his truck?"

"It broke down."

"You're not taking my car tonight."

"I know. You told me that."

"Well, I'm telling you again."

"We don't need it anyway because we're going over to Harry's Tavern."

"Then what? Come back here drunk and harass me?"

"No."

"Don't come back if you're going to come back drunk."

I sat down at the kitchen table. Then I looked up at the bare light bulb where the ceiling globe used to be.

"I still don't understand why you're going out drinking with him, especially after what you told me." Mom raised her voice a couple of decibels to compensate for the great gulf between her in the living room and me in the kitchen, though it was basically one very long room.

"Well?" she asked.

"I don't know."

"Why don't you call up some of your other friends?"

"What other friends?"

Mom reached over to the TV and turned it down.

"When are you going to go back to college?"

"I don't know."

"You only took two courses and then you dropped out."

"I didn't like it."

"You better hurry up and make up your mind while you can still collect on your father's Social Security. When you hit 23 you'll have to pay for it yourself."

I didn't respond.

"Will you stop pacing," she ordered.

"I'm not pacing."

"Yes, you are."

"No, I'm not."

"What do you call it?"

"I'm thinking."

"Thinking about what?"

"About why I decided to get together with Jim tonight."

"Why did you?"

"I guess it's because we're like brothers, we've known each other a long time."

"What did you say?"

I heard a car rumble down the street. I walked into the living room to part the curtains in the window beside the TV set.

"Is that them?"

"I'm not sure."

"I want you to do something for me before you go drinking."

"What?"

"I want you stop over to your aunt's and drop off the money for some *Avon* I'm ordering."

"Can't you do that?"

"Why can't you do that for me?"

As many times as I'd heard her say those lines, and in that same pleading sing-song tone of voice, this time she really touched me. "Yes," I said, drawing out the word.

Then the back door opened. Someone stepped into the entryway, then knocked at the door.

"Come on in," I shouted.

"Why don't you go over and open it?" Mom asked.

The door opened.

Jim looked fresh, clean-shaven, neat, as if he'd recently changed out of a suit. Then I noticed his wedding band. I wondered what Pam would think of that.

"Is Debra coming in?" Mom asked him, still setting on the couch, glancing at him one moment and at the TV the next.

"No, Mrs. Allrich. She had to go to work."

"How's she doing anyway?"

"All right." Then he spoke to me. "You ready to go?"

"As soon as I put my shoes on."

"Don't forget my *Avon*."

I ignored her.

"You hear me?"

Nothing.

"I said, don't forget my *Avon*."

Then she bolted off the couch. The walls reverberated with her footfalls. Jim watched her cross the floor as she passed between us, grabbing the envelope off the counter and handing it to me.

"Don't forget my *Avon*," she said.

"All right," I said. "I wasn't going to forget it."

"Then acknowledge me."

"Your mother's like a banshee," Jim observed after the storm door slammed behind us.

"She's all right."

"Where we going?"

"We have to stop at Darlene and John's to drop off some *Avon* money."

"Who's Darlene and John?"

"My aunt and uncle."

"Couldn't you do that before I came?"

Maplewood is a small town with houses one on top of the other like a misplaced New England fishing village, only dilapidated, and without the artsy fartsy shops or the tourist money. The town is laid out with only two cross streets, one at each end of a dozen or more long streets. To cut time going from Beachtree Circle to the post office, for example, a person could wend his way through a series of back alleys, if the residents hadn't blocked the way with a fence. Same if a person went to Harry's, only to get there it was necessary to leave the village and pass through the woods along a path hewn out by the village drunks.

"How much farther?"

"The next street."

Darlene and John lived on the top floor of a three-story house sided with gray asbestos shingles. I rang the doorbell.

"I bet John answers the door," I said.

"Why?"

"Because Darlene tells him to."

We heard footfalls getting closer, saw the curtains part for a moment, heard the inside door unlatch and then open with a swoosh. John stood almost as tall as the door.

"Mom wanted me to drop off her *Avon* money," I said to John.

"Darlene," John yelled up the stairs.

"What," she yelled back.

"Kevin's here with his mother's *Avon* money."

"Have him come up."

"Jim and I are going to Harry's for a beer, and we don't have time to stop in."

"Oh no. You're going to have to give it to Darlene personally. I'm not going through that again."

"What again?"

"Her accusing me of stealing her *Avon* money."

"Can't I give it to you?"

"Nope. Besides, I'll give you a beer."

"You wanna go up?" Jim shrugged and looked away. Why didn't he say he didn't want to go up? The freaking liar.

We followed John up a very steep flight of stairs and, at the threshold, John had to duck his dirty blond head. The guy must have towered six foot-six, six foot-eight. The house smelled like a wet towel dug from the bottom of a laundry hamper overlaid with a hint of lilac.

"I'll be out in a minute," Darlene yelled through the bathroom door.

John rooted through the refrigerator. "What do you want to drink?"

"I'll have a beer," I said.

"What about you?"

"This is my friend Jim."

"What about you, Jim?"

"I'll take a beer if you're giving them away."

By the time Darlene emerged from the bathroom, the three of us had started a second beer. Our conversation halted when she entered the room. We heard a loud ding ding ding from the TV blaring in the background—the same game show Mom usually watched at this time in the evening. Someone had won a car.

"Oh, hello," she said.

She had long brown hair that parted in the middle and flipped up at the ends, like a beauty pageant contestant from the state of Texas, but her squat nose looked like the nail-prying butt end of an ax, which spoiled her beauty.

"Mom wanted me to drop off her *Avon* money," I said.

"Where is it?"

"Don't worry," John said. "It's on the table at the top of the stairs."

"Where?" she asked, leaving the room. "Oh. I found it." We listened to her tear open the envelope. "How much is supposed to be there?"

"I don't know," I said. "There's a receipt or something."

"Oh, yeah." She flipped through the dollar bills as she came back into the room, then emptied the change into the palm of her hand. "Okay." She looked up at us. "Listen. My program's on in 20 minutes."

"We're almost done," I said.

"You're staying for another one, aren't you guys?"

Jim looked at me like a trapped animal.

"Isn't that all the beer we have?" Darlene asked John.

"So what?"

"It doesn't grow on trees."

Jim leaned over to me as the two went at it about the beer. "Let's get the hell out of here," he whispered.

John got up and marched to the fridge as if somehow he were in charge.

"We're having another beer," he said.

"It's all right, Uncle John," I said. "Forget it. We have to get going." But before I could finish the sentence, he flipped open a beer cap and started on the second.

"Too late," he said, then handed one to each of us.

"You having one, hon?"

She ignored him.

"Aunt Darlene, Jim got married last Saturday," I said, I don't know why.

"Really?" she said. "That's wonderful. When?"

"Three days ago," Jim said.

"Why aren't you on your honeymoon?"

"We stayed one night in Niagara Falls. That's enough."

"Jim and Debra have lived together for almost two years," I proffered.

"Oh."

"That explains it," John said.

"Explains what?" Darlene asked.

"Not needing more than one day to get your jollies."

Jim leaned over to me again and whispered, "Let's get the hell out of here."

"Listen," I said. "Jim and I have to get going."

"I hate to be rude, but my program's on in five minutes."

"Wait," John said. "Before you leave I want to ask if you can figure out a math problem from work."

"What problem?" I asked.

"This drafting equation."

John carefully wrote down a series of numbers while Darlene flipped the channel knob on the TV set.

"Take a look," John said. "You've had algebra. You think you could solve that with algebra?"

"I don't know," I said.

"You took an algebra course at college, didn't you?" John asked.

"That was two years ago, before I dropped out."

"Well, take a look. My buddy at work says you need calculus to solve it."

"I've never studied calculus."

"Let me see," Jim said. He pawed the paper and looked at it like he didn't want to look at it. "You can't solve that," he said to me.

"Come on you guys," Darlene said. "Two more minutes."

"Let me see it again." This time I really looked. "Gimme a pencil."

"Well?" John asked.

"Wait a minute."

"You're fooling yourself," Jim said.

"No. Wait."

"Come on," Darlene said.

"Almost there."

"Maybe you do need calculus," John said.

"No. Wait." I kept scribbling calculations with the pencil. "Is the answer two?"

"Wow," John said.

"Get out," Jim said.

"Is it really two?" I asked.

"I knew you could do it without calculus. It's that my buddy couldn't do it."

"Finally your college education is good for something," Jim said.

"Well, you couldn't do it," I said.

"Big deal."

"No," John said. "That's pretty good."

"All right, let's get the hell out of here," Jim said. "I'm thirsty."

"Let me get you another one."

"John, my program has started."

As we headed along the path through the woods on the way to Harry's Tavern, Jim said, "Your family's crazy."

"What makes you say that?" I asked, but what I was thinking was, no more freaking crazy than you.

"That Darlene was a trip."

"She's all right."

"She's totally pussywhipped him. He's like a broke down cur we used to have on the farm." He did his imitation of a frightened cur. I didn't say anything.

"How do you know your way through the woods?" Jim asked. "You can barely see your hand in front of your face."

"Look through the trees and follow the lights to Harry's Tavern."

"Fuck," Jim said.

"What?"

"I got a branch in my balls."

Chapter 11

Harry's Tavern was not my favorite bar; it had no class. But maybe it was the perfect bar for me. I had no class. So what if it smelled of stale beer and old smoke? So what if the carpet had holes worn through to the floor? So what if they had no top-shelf whiskey and only one beer on tap? So what if most of the pool cues had broken tips, and the green velvet was frayed in the pockets? What did I have? A kitchen with a busted ceiling globe, a freaking pigsty for a bedroom, and a couple of freaking drunks for friends? I didn't even have a freaking car. But at least I aspired to class (whatever class was). Something deep down inside made me think I was better than Harry's Tavern. Maybe I was better than Jim, too.

"I'll get the first round," I said. "It's a wedding gift."

"Don't start that," Jim said.

"Start what?"

"Let's play some pool." Jim began to rack up the balls. "You wanna break?"

"No, go ahead."

By the third beer my cue arm followed through, and balls fell into the pockets with authority. This did not happen sober. Neither pool nor talking to girls was something I did well sober. The opposite seemed to happen to Jim. At one point, I knocked in five in a row, but his four that he left on the table made it difficult for me to take a clear shot at the eight ball. Still, I did, and sunk it."

"You sonofabitch," Jim said.

"Sorry."

"But you know what they say?"

"What?"

"Lucky in pool; unlucky in love."

That stung. What a bastard. "How was the wedding?"

"I don't want to talk about it."

"Why not?"

"Nothing to talk about."

"Well maybe if I'd gone I wouldn't have to ask you."

He took a sip of his beer.

"So?"

"So?"

"So what happened?"

"That family of hers is nuts."

"What else?"

"The usual. Whatever happens at a wedding."

"Forget it. I'll ask Deb tomorrow."

"You do that."

I'd only finished half my fourth when Jim purchased his fifth and quickly downed it, taking long draughts. His pool really got sloppy after that. He tried to match this smooth stroke of mine that sent the five in the corner. The cue ball underspinned and stayed put, setting up my next shot. In his similar attempt, the cue ball flew off the table and bounced under a bar stool.

"I thought you had a better aim than that?"

"Fuck you," he said under his breath.

"What?"

"I'll show you what kind of aim I have."

"What do you mean?"

"One college course didn't make you too bright."

"I took two college courses and I still don't get what you mean."

"Forget it. You want another?"

"I'm still working on this one. Besides, I don't want to get too drunk."

"Why?"

"I don't, that's all," I said, but what I thought was, because Mom had told me not to come home if I was going to come home drunk. I didn't want to say that to Jim.

"I don't want to stay too sober," Jim said.

"Why?"

"Because I have to go home to that bitch."

"Is that what you really think of Deb?"

"Yes." He took a sip. "No." He shook his head. "I don't know. Pam called me today."

"When?"

"This morning."

"What did she say?"

"What do you think she said?"

"You're not going to still see her are you?" He did his usual avoidance routine, looking off in another direction and taking a swig of beer. "Are you?"

"I already have, you dumb fuck."

Jim slid off the bar stool and used the pool cue to stand straight. I sat down at the bar, took a swig and watched him take a shot. He missed another easy one.

"Who's a dumb fuck?" I asked.

"Huh?"

"I don't appreciate being called a dumb fuck."

"What?"

"You just called me a dumb fuck."

"When?"

"A minute ago."

"Oh."

"There's something I want to ask you."

"What?"

"Why did you freakin' lie to me about me having to be the head cook on your wedding day?"

"I didn't lie."

"Yes, you did."

"Nope."

"That's not what Princess said."

"What did Princess say?"

"That you told Tony to tell me he needed me at the restaurant even though he didn't."

"That's a lie."

"Is it?"

"Yeah."

"Tony did most of the cooking, and Princess said she could have done my job, which she's done before."

"So?"

"That's all you're going to say?"

"There's nothing to say."

"Isn't there?"

"No."

"You're a liar."

"No, I'm not."

"Your whole life is a freakin' lie. If you'd lie to Deb you'd lie to me."

"Hey," someone behind us said.

"Do I have to take this shit from you, too?" Jim asked.

"What shit?"

"Hey, you two," someone said again.

"This grilling."

"What grilling?"

"Where I've been. Where I'm going. What did I do. Why did I do it."

"Take it outside," said the voice again, this time louder than the bar din. I looked over to see the pimply-faced bartender pointing to us.

"What?" I asked.

"If you're going to fight, take it out to the parking lot."

"What do you mean?"

"You heard me."

"What time is it?" Jim asked.

"Why? You gotta date with Pam?"

"No, you dumb fuck."

"It's 11:15."

"Why didn't you tell me?"

"Tell you what?"

"That it was after 11."

"What difference does that make?"

"Deb's picking me up at 11."

"I don't see why that should matter."

"Let's go," Jim said.

I should have stayed. The tug of another beer was almost strong enough to keep me in that dingy room, illuminated by the light dangling over the pool table. What perversity made me exit the door with him? But I did, and I kept needling him.

"What difference does it make if Deb's going to be there?" I asked, rephrasing my question which seemed to have been spoken in a vacuum. The words sounded different outside after the door had closed, without the clinking of glass or the voices of a dozen loudmouths. He ignored me. "I can't believe you've seen Pam already."

We walked slowly through the mostly empty parking lot to the alley. Across the road was Maplewood Lake, this dark, forlorn puddle surrounded by black willows hanging their branches over the water. I also saw a few cottages and an occasional light. Behind the tavern stood the woods, mostly tall maples and beaches and taller hemlocks.

"Well?" I asked.

"Well what?"

"You're still seeing Pam?"

"It's none of your business."

"You just said you were."

"So?"

"So?"

"So what?"

"I can't believe it. Why the freakin' hell did you get married?"

He said nothing.

"It would kill Deb if she knew."

That's when he shoved me. I think. That's when I think he tried to turn me around to punch me. But I'm not sure. The next minute I had him on the ground, or he had me on the ground, wrestling. We rolled in a mud puddle. We didn't talk, we grunted. I heard him breathing hard. I knew he could beat me, so I broke free and ran straight into the woods where I knew he couldn't follow.

"Come back here," he said, chasing or following me to the wood's edge. "What the fuck?"

But by then I was running freaking fast, like a deer crashing through brush, jumping dead logs, running, running.

I knew he couldn't make it back to the house before I could, even if he ran at top speed. Even if he started from point A to point B, and I started from point C to point B, and these two points were equidistant, he couldn't beat me. But we'd both started from point A towards point B, but I in something of a straight line, and he in something of an arc. But why should I go to point B?

When I got to my house, I took a moment to scope out the place through the living room window. By the flashing gray TV light I could see Mom and Debra sitting on the couch. How long had Debra sat there? Debra took a drag off her cigarette, then Mom reached over to the ashtray and did the same. I opened the door.

"Where have you been?" Debra asked.

I walked straight through the kitchen, past the bathroom, and up the stairs.

"That's not very nice to keep Debra waiting," the foghorn added.

"Gimme a minute," I yelled down the stairwell. I looked at myself in the hallway mirror and watched myself strip off the muddy clothes down to my underpants. Why couldn't I do something about my puny arms and sunken chest, damn it? Then I dressed. As I closed the top button on a fresh shirt, Jim arrived. I heard muted voices, and then his, clearly, "Is he here?" And then my mother, the trumpet, "Kevin?" And again, "Kevin?"

"What?" I shouted down the stairs, my own voice bouncing off the plaster and the bare hardwood steps. Jim appeared at the bottom of the stairs, much muddier than I was, hair matted to his forehead. He looked up at me, eyes like slits, ready to pounce. I looked down at him with a wide-eyed what-did-I-do look. Then Debra appeared, tenderly grabbing his arm. She looked at me with a what-the-heck-happened look. Jim said, "Let's go."

I laid down on my bed and strained my ears. For a few more minutes I heard their muted voices, then silence, then the car door slam and the engine rev up. I followed the sound of the car down the street and fade out. Then I waited, wondering when I'd hear Mom's penetrating voice try to pry out an explanation. But she left me alone.

Chapter 12

I awoke the next afternoon; no siren call from Mom telling me I was sleeping half my life away, no pounding on the bathroom door because I was spending too much time in the shower. What the heck was going on?

Timmy sat at the table eating lunch. Had he really managed to awaken before me? I poured milk on a bowl of cereal.

"You almost done with the paper?" I asked him. He handed me the section he'd already read.

"What's the matter, you're not talking?" He turned the newspaper page as he took a bite of his sandwich.

"Is that liverwurst?" I asked. I could see that it was. "How can you stand that stuff?"

"Let me finish watching my program," Mom said. "That's all I ask."

"It's OK," Timmy answered.

"I never liked it."

"OK, you two. Knock it off. Give me ten more minutes."

"I swear," Timmy said. "She makes things worse than they really are."

"You got that right."

"You two finish eating and leave me with my program."

"We're only talking about liverwurst," I said.

"Whatever you're talking about, it's too loud."

Timmy lowered his voice. "Was that you and Jim in the parking lot of Harry's Tavern last night?"

"When?"

"Last night."

"I mean, when last night?"

"I don't know."

"What did you see?"

"That *was* you and Jim?"

"What did you see?"

"Were you guys wrestling?"

"More than that."

"What were you doing?"

"Fighting."

"Fighting?"

"Yeah."

"Like you would have a chance against Jim."

"I don't know. I gave him a run for his money."

"You mean you ran."

"What exactly did you see?"

"I don't know."

"It sounds like you do know."

"Give me five more minutes," Mom said. Timmy lowered his voice again.

"She's like a banshee," he said.

"That's what Jim said yesterday."

"What business is it of his?"

"I don't know."

"You should've kicked his teeth in."

"Why? He's a friend of mine."

"If he's a friend, why were you fighting?"

"I don't know."

"Who's fighting?" Mom asked, pivoting her large frame in our direction while heaving out a massive cloud of smoke.

"When are you going to stop smoking?" I asked.

"Yeah," Timmy agreed.

"When you two stop harping at me about it."

"But even if we don't say anything, you still do it," I said.

"Don't start with me."

"We're not starting," Timmy said. "We're concerned about your health."

"If you're that concerned about my health, why did you put me in the hospital?"

"We didn't put you in the hospital," I said.

"I still have the stitches to prove it."

"But you weren't in the hospital," I said.

"I was in the emergency room."

"But you didn't stay overnight in the hospital," I said.

"I didn't say that I did."

"Oh, brother," I said.

"Give me two more minutes."

She pivoted back, leaned over, and ratcheted up the volume knob. I turned to my brother. "Where were you? What did you see?"

"Forget it," Timmy said.

"No. What did you see?"

"Nothing."

"Nothing? It sounds like you saw something." He didn't respond. "Well?" I asked.

My brother ate the last piece of liverwurst from the sandwich but put the uneaten corners of two slices of bread on his plate. He said, with his mouth full, "You and Jim fighting."

"Where were you?"

"In a van."

"Where?"

"Pulling into the parking lot."

"In what van?"

"Rodney's van."

"You saw me fighting and didn't get out of the car and help me?"

"Knock it off," Mom said. She took my rising decibel level as a cue to turn down the TV and bound into the kitchen. "Knock it off, you two."

"Must be your program's over," I said.

"If I want to spend my whole day watching soap operas, I'll spend it watching soap operas. It's my goddamn house."

"All right," I said.

"And by the way," she added, "you smell like a distillery."

"What do you mean?"

"It's obnoxious."

"I had a few drinks last night. So what?"

"That's all you two know how to do, get drunk?"

"I didn't drink yesterday," Timmy said.

"I thought you said you were in the driveway of Harry's Tavern," I said.

"So?"

"So you didn't go in?"

"No."

"Right," I said.

"Mom, he got into a fight last night," Timmy said.

"With who?"

"Forget it," I said to my brother.

"Jim."

"Jim?" Mom asked.

"It was nothing. We were wrestling."

"You said you were fighting," Timmy said.

"Why didn't you get out of the car and help me?"

"I thought about it. But by the time I was ready to get out, you were running into the woods."

"What did Jim do?" I asked.

"He went into the woods, came out a minute later, stood there shaking his goddamn fist, and then ran like hell down the road."

"Uh, watch your language," Mom said.

"OK."

"What were you two fighting about?" Mom asked.

"I don't know."

"It must've been about something."

"I beat him at pool, I think. I can't remember."

"Well, that goddamn troublemaker better not come back in this house," Mom said.

"Why not?"

"Didn't you say you got into a fight with him?"

"But I have to work with him."

"I don't care. He's not coming in here."

"Don't bring him to another party either," Timmy said.

"Why?"

"Because he puked all over the back of Rodney's van."

"Quiet," Mom said.

"Why?" I asked.

"Shhhh."

Then my brother and I could hear what Mom's super-sensitive radar ears had already detected. Someone had opened the entryway door and had stepped inside. We became silent and waited for the knock.

"Come on in," Mom yelled. Now if I had yelled that, she'd have reprimanded me, but she owned the house; she made the rules. It was Debra.

The lower part of her face smiled, but the upper hid another expression which I couldn't figure out.

"Are you busy?" Debra asked me.

"No, not really."

"You wanna go for a ride, maybe grab a bite to eat?"

"Right now?"

Then Mom intervened. "Are you all right, Debra?"

"Oh, yeah."

"Are you sure?"

"Everything's great." She turned to me again. "You wanna go?"

I heaved one of my classic sighs. "Okay. I've already had a bowl of cereal, but I could probably eat some more. Let me get my shoes on." I looked by the door. No shoes. I looked by the heater. Nope. "Hold on." I ran upstairs, looked by the bed, the chair, under the bed, by the chair again, behind the chair. Where were those freaking shoes? "Mom, have you seen my shoes?" I yelled down the stairs.

"I don't wear your shoes."

"You might have put them someplace."

"I didn't touch your shoes."

"You sure you didn't move them when you were cleaning?"

I looked on the stairs, in the bathroom, by the heater again. "Are you sure?"

"I told you I didn't touch your goddamn shoes."

"Hold on, Deb," I said as I brushed past her.

"Phew," Debra said. "You stink."

"Isn't that awful?" Mom agreed.

"Am I that bad?"

"Yep," Debra said. "You better chew some gum or something."

"And change your clothes," Mom said.

"How about you stop drinking," Timmy added.

"You should talk."

"Don't start," Mom said.

"For God's sake," I said. "Here they are."

"Where?" Mom asked.

"By the door, under the throw rug."

"Jesus Christ," Mom said. "Why don't you look once in a while?"

When we passed through the outer storm door, I said, "What a freakin' madhouse."

"Yeah, and you're one of the residents," Debra said.

Chapter 13

"Where are we going?" I finally asked Debra. We were already heading down Hadleyburg-Pomfret Road on the way to Hadleyburg.

"Hadleyburg."

"Why Hadleyburg?"

"Why not?"

"We going drinking?"

"No."

The way she said it shut me up. But I didn't want to talk much anyway. My stomach felt queasy. Maybe I was still a little drunk. She didn't talk either; mostly, she stared straight ahead, hands clenched on the steering wheel, sometimes stealing a look at me as if she wanted to say something. About the third or fourth time she looked at me, I finally had to break the silent spell.

"Well?"

She glanced at me again and took a corner too fast. I looked at a small, chewed-up pasture and at a single cow grazing on a short-clipped clump of greenery. Then we hit a straight stretch of road, wooded on both sides, where I once saw this guy deer-hunting out of his car, pointing a shotgun out of the window while I hung back on my bicycle and waited for the idiot to take a shot and move on.

Finally, on this shadowy stretch, Debra said my name, "Kevin," but the first time she said it, maybe because her throat was dry, half the word got lopped off. She cleared her throat and said it again, "Kevin?"

"What?"

She let out a huge breath which made me look at her bulging belly. "There's something I want to ask you."

"Is this about last night?"

"Last night?"

"You know, about Jim and me fighting last night."

"No."

"Then what?"

Silence again, and another bend in the road.

"I want you to be honest with me."

More silence, and then we passed this still pond reflecting a perfectly blue, post-peak autumn sky.

"Is Jim having an affair?"

"An affair?"

"You heard me."

"Ask him."

"I did."

"What did he say?"

"He said he's not."

"Why ask me?"

"I found this letter in his pants pocket when I was doing his laundry."

I unfolded the pink stationery:

*i love you and you know she can never
love you like i love you. i need you and i
need to see you and i need to speak to
you please call me*

love

Pam

She'd dotted all the "i's" with hearts.

"Is Jim having an affair?"

I couldn't breathe. I cracked the window enough to let a stream of cold air hit my face and looked off into a field. This was it.

"Yes," I said, my breath steaming up the window on the passenger-side door.

"What?"

"I said yes, Jim is having an affair." Debra began to sob. Then we veered off the road into a field and she brought the car to a halt. She turned off the engine.

"How long have they been seeing each other?"

"I don't know."

"How long have you known?"

I didn't answer.

"One week? One month?"

"I was the last person at work to find out."

"You mean everybody there knows?"

I didn't want to talk anymore.

"It's that Pam bitch at work?"

"You know Pam?"

"I met her once. She's a mousy little thing."

"She's not a bitch."

"What?"

"I mean, I—it's not her fault. She's still in high school, for chrissake."

Chapter 14

Twenty, thirty minutes after the time Jim was supposed to pick me up for work, I realized he wasn't coming. I don't know what made me think he would. First I called the farmhouse, and it rang and rang. Then I dialed the restaurant to let them know I'd be late. Tony answered.

"I don't know when I'm going to make it in. I'm waiting for Jim."

"He's already here," Tony said.

"He is?"

"Yep."

"Jesus. He's supposed to pick me up."

"Well, I don't know about that. Try to get in as soon as you can." The dense fog Mom often accused me of living in lifted.

I waited for Mom to return from her part-time job at the nursing home and begged to use her car. At first she said she'd drive me, but then I explained that she'd have to drive back again to pick me up.

"Well Okay, but you'd better start figuring out some other arrangement for the future," she said as I grabbed the car keys.

"I'll freakin' hitchhike if I have to," I said and closed the door, perhaps a little too hard.

Mom's final words: "How many times do I have to tell you not to slam the goddamn door?"

On the ride over, I had an imaginary conversation with the bastard, telling him off, banging my hand on the steering wheel a couple of times, then turning up the radio when a favorite song came on and singing along as loud as I could.

I trembled when I opened the screen door into the kitchen, the way I tremble when I've awakened after a night of heavy drinking. Jim stood, back to the door, stirring the stock pot on the stove. Someone else stood at my station in front of the fryers. When I walked around the center counter out of the way of the hanging pots, I could see Don, of all people, wearing his freaking loafers and a pair of creased pants. Peaking over the top of his apron was the collar of an oxford shirt.

Jim glanced at me, didn't speak though. I said, "Hey," but the word got lost in a clatter of dishes.

"Everything set up?" I asked Don, or maybe Jim, if he'd answer me.

Don replied though. "I believe you'll find everything set up according to the check list Jim prepared. However, I'm not sure that this is the correct consistency of the beer batter."

"You're helping me out tonight or what?"

"I'm in training as a back-up," he said "That's my status according to Tony. Isn't that right, Jim?"

Jim had stopped his busy work and turned toward us, tong in hand, opening and closing it like a lobster claw. But he looked at Don when he finally spoke.

"Yep," he said.

"Why?" I said, starting to tremble.

"If you can't make it to work," Jim said.

"Why wouldn't I make it to work?"

"How you gonna get here?" he asked.

Then, I don't know why, I said it. It shouldn't have been said, but I couldn't stop myself from saying it: "Riding with you, right?"

"You gotta be kidding," he said, like he relished saying it. Lousy bastard. How would I get to work?

Tony entered the kitchen, heading toward me but looking at Jim. His hip knocked into the counter, rattling the hanging pots.

"You tell him?" Tony asked Jim.

"Nope."

"Tell me what?"

"You're in charge of all the employee meals from now on," Tony ordered.

"What do you mean?"

"Can't you hear?" Tony asked me. "From now on I want you to take care of the employee meals."

"Why?"

"Good for you to get some practice cooking, right?"

"I guess so."

"Besides, it's hard for Jim to get his station prepped when he's interrupted by having to cook employee meals."

"What about when I'm prepping my station?"

"It's not a problem for you is it?" Tony asked.

Why was Jim doing this to me, I was thinking, but Tony thought I must have been pondering his question.

"Well?"

"No, I guess not." I said. "No problem."

"So, Don," I said, turning to him. "I guess you better pay attention. You'll have to do this too if I'm not here."

"I'll certainly try to do what I can," Don said.

But Jim cut his sentence short. "No, he won't."

"Won't he?"

"Nope."

"Why not?"

"When you're not here, I'll be doing it."

I ducked into the walk-in to see what else I needed and also to cool off. I kept turning, trying to make up my mind what to do. I diddled around with boxes of produce mostly, opening the tops and then folding them one flap inside another. As I closed up a case of Canadian beer, the lousy bastard came in and grabbed a bunch of parsley. I tried to ignore him, but before he left he turned to me and said, "You're not drinking in here, I hope?"

I didn't speak.

"Well?"

I wouldn't respond.

"Because if I catch you drinking, your ass is out of here."

When I came out of the walk-in, Pam stood, back against the wall on his side of the kitchen. He had her boxed in, like he was doing a push-up against her, their faces very close. They whispered.

Pam glanced at me for a fraction of an instant. She pulled Jim to the side behind the counter, barely out of eyeshot, as if I would keep tabs on them, as if I would care.

Then Brenda turned in the first order of the night, three fish frys and a sirloin steak.

"Order up," Brenda said.

As I tried to pick up the ticket, Jim broke from his dalliance, took two long strides across the rubber mat, and grabbed the order with his tongs.

"Hold it," he said.

"Why?" I asked. "I can read."

"I said, hold it. From now on, I'll tell you what you have to do."

"He's a grouch," Brenda said, sliding half her body over the counter. "Who's that?" Brenda whispered to me, looking at Don. "Are you leaving us?"

"Not that I know of," I said.

"Get those fish down," Jim said.

"Okay," I said.

"Like I said, he's a grouch."

"Get off the counter," Jim ordered. Brenda slid back and stepped around my side of the counter to whisper.

"What's going on?"

"What do you mean?"

"Who is that?" Brenda asked, nodding her head in Don's direction.

"Jim's friend."

"Why is he here?"

"He'll back me up when I can't be here."

"Careful not to teach him everything you know."

"What do you mean?"

"You're so green, you could live in a forest."

"I said, get the fuckin' fish down," Jim ordered.

"All right, all right," I replied.

"Brenda," Tony yelled down the hall from the dining room.

"Coming," she yelled back.

What a freaking busy night it turned into, unusual for a Thursday. At least four tickets at any given time. And usually Don stood right in my freaking way. I wanted to tell him to move. I almost told him a couple of times, but I heaved one of those classic sighs and stepped around him. Jim would have jumped on me for saying anything. Occasionally, Don sidled over to Jim and stood, arms akimbo, asking Jim a question—like how he could tell a medium-rare steak from a well-done steak by touching it, a skill Jim bragged he had.

When Pam appeared, which she did a couple of times that night, she entered the kitchen from Jim's side of the counter, not once talking to me. She always found time to break away from her duties in the pantry to talk to Jim.

At about 8:45 the house went dead, as if all the customers had fled en masse, probably to watch some special TV show. Jim began to break down his station, but he did something I'd never seen him do. He took all of his knives, dumped them into the deep sink on my side of the kitchen, turned on the hot water, squeezed in some detergent, and filled it up. Then he said to me, "From now on you're going to be doing most of the cleanup around here."

"Uh huh."

"And it starts with the knives."

"I'm not putting my hands in that water. I can't even see those knives."

"So what?"

"I don't mind doing the knives, but you can't put them in soapy water. I can't see where the blades are."

"Are you a man or a wimp?"

"It has nothing to do with whether or not I'm a wimp. I'm not stupid."

"I don't know about that."

"I'm going to talk to Tony."

"Go ahead. I've already talked to him about you doing the cleanup. He doesn't care."

"I don't believe it."

"He said it's my kitchen. I'm the boss."

"Tony's the boss."

"Go ask him."

"Forget it."

"Then wash the knives."

I started to exit the kitchen.

"Where the fuck you going?"

"To take a piss, do you mind?"

I had to leave the kitchen and enter the bar area in order to get to the bathroom. Brenda, standing outside the counter, was wiping the spots off dozens of wine glasses.

Tony, behind the bar, took each one as she finished and hung it over the cash register. As I walked past her, she grabbed my arm.

"There's something I want to tell you."

"About what?"

"About you know who."

"If it's about the lousy bastard in the kitchen, I don't want to hear about it."

"Oh, Okay," she said with mock seriousness. "If you don't care about your reputation, then neither do I." Tony moved to the other end of the bar to get a customer a beer.

"What do you mean?"

"It's about something Jim said earlier."

"About me?"

"Yes."

"What is he going to say about me? What have I done compared to what that asshole has done?"

She stared at me, wrinkled her forehead, and let me keep talking.

"I mean, that sonofabitch is in there slobbering all over Pam, and meanwhile he got married and his wife is going to have a baby. What kind of bullshit is that? "

Tony came back and hung glasses again.

"Well, to hear Jim talk, what kind of bullshit are you up to?" Brenda asked.

"You mean because his wife finally asked me if he was having an affair, and I told her it was true?"

Tony stopped hanging glasses and started listening.

"No. He said that you've been sleeping with Debra and that's probably your kid she's carrying."

"He said that?"

"Didn't he, Tony?"

Tony gave me a sad-eyed-dog look and then let out a "Yep."

I let out an audible breath, shook my head, and tried to think what to say. If I protested too much, it might sound like it was true, and if I protested too little, they might think the same.

"He's freakin' slick," I finally said. "He is smooth. Is that what you guys think?"

Brenda giggled. "No."

"What's so funny?" I asked.

"I think you're a virgin."

I'm sure my face turned about as red as it could. I couldn't look at her after she said that. All I could do was turn and head back to the kitchen. I may have wiped away a tear. She tried to stop me by grabbing my shirtsleeve. "You're not mad at me are you?" But I didn't stop.

When I returned to the kitchen, Pam sat on the counter and Jim was running his hand along her inner thigh.

"Get those knives washed," Jim said.

But I turned toward him and looked straight into his freaking eyes and said: "Did you tell everyone here that I'm sleeping with Debra?"

That stunned him for a minute.

"I said, did you tell everyone here that I'm sleeping with Debra?"

"Well, you are," Pam said. Tony and Brenda and a couple of the other waitresses came into the kitchen. I ignored Pam.

"You gonna deny you said it?" Jim still didn't speak. "You're a freakin' liar and you know it. How could anyone believe anything you said, you liar. You got your freakin' wife pregnant, and you're freakin' cheating on her and you know it."

"That's your child," Pam said.

"Is that what he told you? You believe him? He's a freakin' liar."

"I think you better finish breaking down the kitchen," Jim finally said.

"That's why I call you Occy," Pam said. "Because you have eight arms when it comes to girls."

"You bitch," I said to her. Jim moved toward me.

"Get away from me," I said.

"What are you going to do?"

"I'll grab one of those knives."

"I thought you were afraid to put your hands in the water?"

He took another step toward me. I started to reach in the water. He grabbed my wrist as my fingertips broke the surface, and then squeezed hard. Then he tried to twist my arm behind my back.

"Let go of me."

"Let go of him," Tony said. I broke free.

"Asshole," I said to him.

"Get the fuck out of here and don't come back," Jim said to me.

"You can't fire me. Can he Tony?"

Tony couldn't look at me. Even Brenda looked away.

"No," I said. "You can't fire me because I freakin' quit. Get out of my way," I said to Don, who stood between me and the door.

"Bye bye, Occy," Pam said as the door slammed behind me. "Go home and cut your mother's other foot."

Chapter 15

Debra called the next day blubbering on the other end of the receiver. Would there ever be an end to me being the confidante to the damsel in distress, never the knight in shining armor? I'd shoved two slices of white bread into the toaster.

"What happened?" I asked.

"Jim took something out of the engine so the car won't start."

"How do you know?"

"I saw him close the hood of my car a few minutes before he peeled out of the driveway."

"The bastard."

"He kicked up some stones, and I thought the kitchen window was going to break."

"Hold on," I said. I set the receiver down and grabbed the toast, slathering butter on it as I resumed the conversation.

"Why don't you call the police?"

"I'm afraid."

"Afraid of what?"

"Afraid of what he'd do to me."

"What's he going to do?"

She blew her nose. She sounded like an elephant at a watering hole.

"I don't know," she said, "but that's why I need you to do me a favor. No, I need two favors."

"What?"

"Can you give me a lift to work? I've called the garage, but I don't think they're going to come in time."

I'd taken an oversized bite of toast and for a moment couldn't speak.

"Well?" she asked.

"I'm eating breakfast."

"Oh."

"Mom's at the grocery store. When would you need the ride?"

"About three."

"What's the other favor?"

"Would you take the gun with you?"

"What gun?"

"Jim's shotgun."

"Why?"

"I don't want it in the house."

After I agreed and hung up, I dismissed the idea of taking Jim's gun. I thought her suggestion irrational. She could hide it; she could take the slugs out; she could dismantle it and throw it away; she could call the police.

Before I left for the farmhouse, I swilled three beers. Make that two and 7/8ths. I ditched the last swigs of a third in the trash under the kitchen sink before Mom walked in. I had to duck into the bathroom to brush my teeth before I asked for the car. No problem at all, she said, as long as it helped Debra.

When I rounded the bend and saw the farmhouse and barn, I automatically slowed, surveying the scene. I scanned the highway to see if I could spot Jim's red pickup truck. I couldn't, so I crossed the intersection, drove down the road, and pulled in beside Debra's disabled sedan. I was early.

I thought I would see her standing by the back door ready to go, but instead she unlatched the kitchen window, poked her head through, and told me to come in, which I did.

"I'm running a little late," she said. "I'm waiting for my waitress uniform to dry. After I got off the phone with you, I realized I didn't have a thing to wear."

"OK."

"Actually, I have some other uniforms but this is the only one that still feels comfortable." She turned sideways and pointed both hands to her belly. She was definitely showing.

"You see what I mean?" she asked.

"How much longer?"

"I don't know, two-and-a-half months."

"No. I mean how much longer before your dress is dry?"

"Five or ten minutes. I put a few other things in the dryer. That's why it's taking a little longer than I thought."

"All right."

"Let me check again."

I watched her extra-wide load exit into the laundry room. No question she was packing on the pounds. She returned with Jim's shotgun, holding it barrel side down, her arm extended as if it might be radioactive.

"Will you take this thing now and stick it in your car?"

"What am I going to do with it?"

"I don't know, but take it."

"And then he comes after me?"

"How's he gonna know?"

"Why don't you hide it or hide the bullets?"

"Because he'll find it. Sooner or later, he's gonna come back when I'm gone and get in."

"Let him take it."

"You're not going to do it for me?"

"I guess. "

"I mean, if you don't want to do that for me, why not say so?"

"I didn't say that."

"Then here." Debra succeeded in doing what Jim couldn't talk me into doing a few weeks before: take the gun in my hands, feel the heft of it, feel the power and control of it.

"Why don't you take it out now?" she asked.

"I will when we go." I laid the gun on the counter. "He was upset today?"

"I'll say. But not as upset as he was two days ago."

We both heard the dryer click off.

"That was quick," she said. "That can't be dry already."

I followed her into the laundry room and watched her try to bend over to check the dryness of the load. She grunted.

"Five to ten more, I think," she said.

"I wish you could have told me you were doing the laundry. I could have started a little later."

"Why? Is that a problem? I mean, you don't mind, do you?"

"No."

She closed the dryer door, set the timer, and restarted it.

"What happened the other day?" I asked.

"What day?"

"The day you asked me about Jim. Remember? We went off the road?"

"Oh, yeah," she said. She sat down on a footstool in the corner and seemed not much more of a heap than the bundle of dirty laundry by the washing machine.

"I called him a liar and told him to pack his bags."

"What did he say?"

"He said I should pack my bags, that this was his farmhouse."

"Did you mention me? Did you say that I'm the one who told you?"

"Not exactly."

"What do you mean?"

"I said that somebody reliable said it was true."

"What did he say?"

"I don't remember."

The dryer suddenly emitted a grating sound that lasted a good 30 seconds.

"That doesn't sound healthy," I said.

"That thing is on its last legs. Ever since Jim jury-rigged it, it makes that sound."

"At least you don't have to drive to the laundromat."

"I do if I want to wash anything."

"How did you wash your dress?"

"By hand in the sink."

"No wonder it's taking this long to dry."

"Hold your horses. Give it a couple more minutes."

"You have a beer or anything?"

"Not cold."

"Where?"

"In the back entryway. It's Jim's stash."

"If it's out there, it'll be cool at least."

I passed through the kitchen door into the entryway and got another whiff of onions and cow shit. I had to step over a few boxes and lift up some coats and a garden rake and nearly had to shout out, "I can't find it," before I spotted the case of *Labatts*. I took two of the three remaining beers, opening one and putting the other inside my jacket pocket. When I returned, she was unfolding an ironing board.

"Aren't you gonna be late?" I asked.

"I can't go to work with a wrinkled dress."

"Speaking of work, they're not hiring at your restaurant, are they?"

"I don't know."

"Aren't you gonna ask me why?"

"I already know why."

"You know that I quit?"

"I thought Jim fired you."

"He told you that?"

"This dress is still damp under the arms," she said. She kept feeling up the dress. Then she turned it inside out. "I think I can iron out the dampness." I took a long swig of beer.

"He really said he fired me?"

"Yeah."

"Bastard."

"I told him you weren't the one who squealed on him, but he said he didn't believe me."

"He didn't?"

"He said who else could have told?"

"What did you say?"

"I said I had the love letters to prove it."

"You mean there was more than one?"

"I found a whole box," she said.

"Where?"

"In the entryway."

"You know, that entryway stinks," I said.

"I think it's a bag of rotting onions."

"Or a dead cow."

"Or something."

"What did he say when you confronted him about those letters?"

"What could he say? I still don't understand what he sees in her. Do you?" I opened the second beer. "Are you finished with that first beer already?"

"Yep."

"Jesus, you and Jim both."

"Both what?"

"Both drink like fish."

"I'd rather not be compared to the bastard. I mean, at least I wasn't fat and didn't wear the same clothes every day when I was in high school."

"What does that have to do with anything?"

I brushed the hair out of my eyes and tried to think what brought me to that trend of thought.

"Well?" she asked.

"Let me think."

"Maybe you've had too much to drink already."

"No, before you asked what Jim saw in Pam, and I have a theory."

"What theory?"

"That he's experiencing the years that he never could experience as a teenager because he was fat and poor and he was a farmer and he never had a freakin' girlfriend, and now some pretty teenager pays him some attention and he goes gaga over her."

"That doesn't make any sense," she said as she turned the dress outside in.

"I think it does. Is that freakin' dress dry yet?"

"I guess so."

At that moment we both heard the storm door creak open, boots clunk on wooden planks, and the storm door spring shut. Then the kitchen door opened. I hadn't bolted it.

"What the fuck are you doing here?" Jim asked, his head facing Debra but his eyes looking at me. Why bother to ask, I thought, since he could see my car parked outside. He looked like he hadn't combed his hair in days.

"You can't keep me from getting my fuckin' clothes. Don't even try, bitch."

"She's not the bitch," I said.

"I wouldn't start," he said. "In fact, why don't you get in your mommy's car and get the fuck out of here?"

I ignored him and took a swig of beer, delighting in knowing that I was drinking his stash but wishing I'd taken the third beer from the case.

"Why don't you get the hell out of here," Debra said, unplugging the iron and moving the ironing board to the side. "Get out and leave me alone."

"Can't you see how much you've hurt her already, for chrissake?" I asked. "Not to mention that baby. And that is your freakin' baby, not mine like you told everyone at work."

"Shut the fuck up."

"Is that what you told everybody?" Debra asked.

Jim had inched his way into the kitchen and now stood between me by the kitchen counter and Debra by the dining room table.

"Let's set the record straight," I said. "Why don't you tell the freakin' truth?"

"Okay. Let's tell the truth," Jim said.

"Okay."

Jim's eyes became slits. "Why don't you tell Debra about our trip to the cabin. Have you told Debra about going out with me and Pam and partying at the cabin?"

"What?" Debra said.

"Pam was all right then, wasn't she? Free food, free booze. She even hooked you up with a girl, and you didn't even kiss her. Jim kept edging closer to me."

"Is that true?" Debra asked me.

"It wasn't like that at all."

"No?" Jim asked.

"No, you're trying to change the freakin' subject because you don't want to accept responsibility for your actions."

"No, I'm not."

That's when I think he shoved me, or poked me. I don't remember. I stepped back, picked up the shotgun, and in a moment I had it pointed at him.

"What are you going to do, fuckin' shoot me?" He looked at me without blinking.

"I'd like to fuckin' shoot you, you fucker."

"Go ahead."

"Fuck you."

"Shoot."

That's when I pulled the trigger. And then I tried to pull the trigger a second time.

And then Jim laughed.

"You fuckin' idiot. There are no slugs in that gun." He grabbed it out of my hands. "You fuckin' waste of a ball sack."

That's when I ran, shot out of the house like a deer running from a hunter, about as fast as I'd ever run, my lungs heaving, hurting from too much smoking and from working them to capacity. I ran into the brush on the other side of the house. That's when I saw his truck and the profile of Pam in the passenger seat. I waited, heart pounding, for 10-15 minutes. He came out with two plastic garbage bags filled with clothes or whatever.

When the truck pulled out, I skulked to the car, half-expecting Debra to stop me and say, "Hey, aren't you gonna take me to work?" But she didn't, so I drove away.

OTHER SAD TALES OF THE APPALACHIAN FOOTHILLS

Bull Derby

So my boys are at it again, Bull Derby thought as he spat a wad of tobacco on the kitchen floor, missing the cat which lazily got up from its sprawling position, sniffed it, didn't like what it smelled, ran into the living room, clawed the back of the couch, and rattled praying Jesus on the window sill. "Damned cat," he said to the Sherriff or to the cat.

"I ain't gonna wipe that up, you pig," Bull's wife yelled from across the room.

"My boys couldn'ta made nobody eat out of a pig trough, Sheriff, unless they wanted to," Bull said as he ran his hand through his crew cut and felt the bald spot with his index finger, made the time he pulled his father's pant leg and his father poured on a ladle of boiling water.

"Well, they done it," the Sheriff said, stepping back into the threshold. "George's boy's lying in the hospital with smashed teeth and potato mash up his sinuses."

A few more words were said as the Sheriff backed off into the entryway and over some missing floor boards, brushing against pickle jars and 10-40 oilcans, down one step, then another, taking a rich whiff of the barn, hearing the cows groaning.

"Like I says, he musta wanted it done," Bull said, seeing red, grabbing hold of the kitchen table, flinging it upward. One of the table legs caught the ceiling globe his wife had won in a Win-go game at the county fair and smashed it.

"Those boys ain't comin' back in this house," he said.

Meanwhile, his boys were setting fire to the fire hall as the townsfolk were settling onto their couches in front of the flickering light of the television. Three minutes after they heard the two high-toned beeps on the half hour, the fire whistle, which Elmer Herst had the good sense to place one hundred feet from the building in that unlikely event, blew.

Most every adult came out of his house at once, running toward the fire hall, or standing in the street in boxer shorts or night robe and curlers, one asking another asking another and so on, "Where is it?" Or sneaking up back alleys to see it, as some of the children did.

Bull was out of the house as fast as anyone, crunching the glass on the kitchen floor with his steel-toed boots, opening the truck door with a force that might have pulled it off the hinges of one of those foreign jobs, and revving up the motor loud enough to wake the chickens.

Just as Bull pulled out of the driveway on the way to the village, his broad-shouldered boys pulled in, the pick-up trucks stopped, and they stared through the bug-smashed windshields, they at their father and vice versa, and the moment suspended like the dust in the front light beams. Bull shook his head back and forth and that's about all that happened until later in Bull's bed.

If Bull would have thought for one moment life was going to be like this raising three boys, going back and forth to work five days a week on treacherous roads in the winter, seeing red spots on his iris hours after he'd turn off the welding torch, raising and slaughtering thirty cattle or more and countless chickens, and tending five acres of cucumbers, he wouldn't have married, he wouldn't have quit school, he wouldn't have had his sisters raise him after both his parents died, he wouldn't have let them take off to California after he got tuberculosis, he wouldn't have met his wife who was volunteering at the hospital, and he wouldn't have been thinking about this as she was vaselining his manhood.

What Happened to Gary Lee

Nobody in town knew what happened to Gary Lee, but the cops had a good idea the Derby boys had something to do with it. They were the kind of boys who'd tie the front legs and the back legs of a live cat to separate cars and take off. Or at least that's what old lady Snyder said she saw them do once, though the cops took that with a grain of salt considering that only the week before they'd found her wandering in the woods for three days on her way to the grocery to buy bread. But it's true just the same.

They did find a book up by the gravel pile, back of the split-level ranch owned by the Mohawk Indians. It was torn beyond recognition, though the identity of the book is not important, only that Gary Lee liked to read; and he was last seen walking up North Street with a book under his arm, which in this town is tantamount to asking for trouble. Nobody here takes a liking to book learning, not since some egghead from Fish and Wildlife Management introduced a French weed that killed off nearly every living bass in Mud Lake; and not since June McCune, the English teacher, was caught with one of the Anderson boys in the janitorial closet at the high school. But neither one of these instances should deter any sentient being from learning since there's no correlation between the pure joy of learning and the way learning is put into use, or so Gary Lee once said.

There is, however, a witness who has a general idea what happened, and if he wasn't afraid for his own life, he could implicate the Derby boys—who once got no more than a slap on the wrist for burning down the garage where the fire truck was kept; and beyond a shadow of a doubt, too, because Gary Lee confessed they were after him.

This witness, who was on his way to hoe the garden, came across Gary Lee in the field reading a book. The identity of that book also remains a mystery to this witness who never did bother to ask him, and never did care to know; and, as a matter of fact, warned Gary Lee in the most sympathetic manner that he shouldn't be reading in public knowing the temperament of the town, and that the Derby boys are always looking for some poor soul to torment.

Gary Lee was the perfect patsy, too. Just his horn-rimmed glasses were enough to ire the most complacent body because they were thick, and seeing his eyes beneath the lenses reminded a person of a carp, which is the most useless fish, having the foulest taste no matter how you cook it, and thriving in spite of the French lake weed incident.

This witness told Gary Lee how the Derby boys once beat his own eyes black, then buried him up to his neck in the quartz and mica gravel pile near the burnt-up garage where he shouted his voice hoarse until the Indians finally heard him, a little while after they shut off the nightly news.

Gary Lee said something perfectly within his character, and it scared this witness into another warning. Gary Lee said, "I'm not going to be picking potatoes or working in the brewery or being a part of an assembly line for the rest of my life." Gary Lee was obviously challenging nature, just as this witness's grandmother often scolded that if you say you're not going to do something, nature has a way of making you do it—which was told to Gary Lee.

Then Gary Lee said, "I don't know what I'm going to do with my life, but, whatever it is I study, it won't have nothing to do with this county, or even this region. Maybe not even this country." He should have been reminded right there and then of Cissy Harris who lost her arm and leg in an automobile accident the summer she studied art history in Italy.

Then Gary Lee told this witness he'd outsmarted the Derbys earlier that day by slipping through a hole in the fence behind the church, a hole those lumbering Derby giants couldn't have hoped to squeeze through and one they wouldn't have known about anyway, being that it was behind the church.

That's about all the evidence this witness could give, which is, in good part, circumstantial, but would be enough of a lead for the police to find that he's buried in the gravel pile.

In any case, it could've been a blessing in disguise, which is the way everyone in town sees it. Anyone who could put up such a fuss when this witness hoed the heads off a brood of newborn mice that had taken up residence in one of the potato mounds was just too sensitive for this world, and it can only be hoped Gary Lee's appreciated in the next, Lord knows.

Agnes

Agnes wallowed in their pity. How nice it felt to have people stop her in the street and be concerned and stare at her mournfully, their voices dripping with sweetness.

"Oh," she said, drawing it out. "My eye has been hurting so much the last few days, and my joints ache so, I can't lay down to have a good night's sleep. I've been sleeping in the reclining chair."

They couldn't help noticing her sunglasses with the one lens broken out for the good eye, and the cotton taped under the lens of the bad one.

"Well, we hope you're feeling better soon."

"God bless you, and thanks for thinking of me," Agnes said, and up the middle of the street she went, one slow step at a time, helped by the aluminum walker. She'd been out more than usual this week and wanted everyone to know about her cataract surgery.

She let out a big grunt maneuvering around a pothole. "Oh Lord," she said out loud. "When are they going to get this pothole fixed?"

"Why don't you go up the other street?" came a little girl's voice from a window.

"Don't talk to your elders that way, little girl."

"Every day you walk up the street and every day you say the same thing, more or less. You oughta know it's there by now."

"I know who you are," Agnes said in her most menacing voice. "And your mother's going to know, if I have my way."

"She already does know. She raised me."

By now, Agnes had turned halfway around and was leaning on the walker with one hand while she waved her finger with the other.

"You know what I mean."

"No. What do you mean?"

"I mean, I'm going to tell your mother."

"My mother thinks you belong in a home and you shouldn't be out on the streets anyway, and one of these days you're going to slip and fall in your house and no one's going to find you for days, or one of these days you're gong to fall asleep and you're going to set the whole town on fire. She says she doesn't know why none of your family takes care of you and why are you wearing your glasses like that? It looks stupid."

Agnes had started walking up the street to the cafe and was grunting around the pothole, angrier than the time she slipped on the icy sidewalk last winter and bruised her ass-end.

At the cafe, she sat with Amos who'd been in and out of the infirmary because of frequent emphysema attacks, but, when he was able enough to come home, he'd put up such a fuss that they were glad to let him out as long as he promised not to smoke around his oxygen tanks. So he'd smoke in the kitchen, lazing around in a nightshirt that hadn't been washed for a week or two, and almost never shaving until he could taste his mustache hairs in his oatmeal. Then he'd shave, and, as long as he looked halfway decent, he'd go to the cafe.

How they loved to talk to each other about their ailments. But today Agnes outshone him since she'd recently had her cataract surgery, and he'd been out of the infirmary for more than two months, and his lungs weren't acting up, and she was mad. The only drawback, of course, was that they'd have to split the pity between the two of them when one of the local folks came in, and it seemed like they were all in that day.

Every one of them got an earful, what with the coffee cups clattering, and Amos hacking between puffs, and Agnes grunting every time she'd reach across the table for sugar. And she was mad, not only about the impertinent little girl, but also about setting in the doctor's office so long. And the numbness stayed in her eye, not three hours, but three days.

"Well, I watched him coming right down at my eye with the tweezers, or whichever he used," Agnes said. "I insisted on saving the cataract, too." Even Amos sat fascinated. "Oh, but my joints have been acting up so. I've been sleeping in the reclining chair for two days now. That hasn't been good for my back."

When Agnes finally paused to take a breath, she caught a snippet of whispering at the corner table occupied by the postmistress and her sister. ". . . in an infirmary . . .," she caught between her groans. She turned her head and listened. ". . . a danger to the community and as far . . ."

"I know who you are," Agnes bellowed, and the clattering stopped. "Your little girl needs her face smacked. She's the most disrespectful thing in the county."

"My little girl?" the postmistress asked.

"Your little girl. She needs her face smacked or her ass whacked. In my day children didn't talk to their elders that way."

"I think you're talking about someone else."

"No, I'm not," and Agnes told the pothole story again, groaning for emphasis.

"My little girl's in school," said the woman as she put her purse on her shoulder to leave, both out of embarrassment and because Agnes's story sounded so genuinely true that she thought perhaps her daughter had played hooky. She'd done it before, knowing her mother didn't get home from her job until long after she got home from school.

Not one person was in moral disagreement with Agnes's feelings except Amos, and she was sure Amos was trying to take away her day in the sun.

"That's Betty Jenkins from South Street," Amos whispered. "I thought you said it happened on your street."

Agnes's face would have gotten red but she had poor blood circulation and hadn't been able to blush since the last time she'd gotten naked with her husband before he died.

"Bless his soul," she said out loud, thinking of him.

Amos walked Agnes home, and she was unnaturally quiet, especially around the pothole. She saw the curtain parted.

"Bless your soul," she said to Amos as he was about to leave her. He gave her a little goose through the back folds of her dress.

"Oh, oh, oh." She laughed with every "oh" getting louder. So heartily did she laugh that a doctor would call it circulatory therapy, and so loudly that an "Oh, oh, oh," came down the street in a spiteful, girlish, sickeningly sweet echo.

Coming To A Head

Joe felt squeezed in by the two women, as squeezed as he felt now, standing between the two horses in their stalls, each trying to put its head into the bucket of grain. He emptied the feed into the bin and pushed them apart and left the stall to attend the little one.

The abscess on the colt's neck had swelled but had not come to a head, and he knew he would have to do something about it. The colt lay on the hay and looked at him, and he knelt and patted its head, and he touched the abscess, and the colt flinched and whimpered.

What I should do, he thought, is shoot you; put the barrel to your forehead like I was about to shoot a pig and shoot you. He thought about a pig he once shot, how it moved its head, how the bullet passed through its ear and into its shoulder, how the pig broke through into the field, how it rushed the electric fence, how it got madder and fiercer, how it took five shots to bring it down, how the bullets wasted so much good meat.

"She's the only reason you're alive," he said softly. "And I'd like to shoot her, too." The colt lifted its head as he brought the bucket to its snout, and it tried to lift itself out of its awkwardness. But Joe patted the colt's flank and soothed it with soft words, and it ate slowly and swallowed slowly.

Joe brought hot water from the house and applied steaming rags to the abscess. The colt whimpered and flies buzzed. Between each application, he looked, he touched, he soothed. It was coming to a head; someone was coming. He heard a car in the driveway. Was Sheila coming to soothe him, to bed him in the hay? He'd told her not to come here.

Joe lanced the abscess with a razor and puss shot on his sleeve and oozed on his fingers, and behind him stood his friend David. The horse whimpered, and David laughed. He laughed because he was eating pumpkin pie.

"How can you eat while I'm doing this?" Joe asked him.

"How can you sleep with another woman when you're married?" David replied. "This pie has nothing to do with that pus, unless I think it does." They laughed at this logic.

"Then you'll have no trouble helping me clean this shitty bedding because it has nothing to do with what I think of you as a friend," Joe said.

They moved the colt from its bedding, and Joe pitchforked the hay into a wheelbarrow, and David wheeled it out back. They spread out new hay, smelled its sweetness and helped the colt to lie on it and left the flies to work on the colt's neck, except one, which Joe caught and flung into a web. David watched the spider wrap the fly, watched its wings flutter in the thicker and thicker webbing but still flutter.

"I thought the spider killed the fly before wrapping it." But David was alone, and his words floated above to the webbed rafters. Joe had gone inside to wash his hands, so he, too, went into the house.

"Help me kill some chickens." Joe said. "I feel like killing chickens."

"I'll watch, but I'm not going to help."

Joe wanted to say "chicken," but he knew it would be a bad joke and he didn't want to waste time hearing his friend say what a bad joke it was. He wanted to see his friend ax a chicken, and know, for once, how it felt, how good it felt.

"I'll pluck it and dress it, but I won't kill it."

Those were the last words wasted until the thud of the ax on the stump, and then Joe laughed, louder than the chicken's last squawk, louder than David's, "Oh, I hate to see that." Blood spurted with its dying heartbeats.

"I'd like to do that to her," Joe said.

David dared say nothing. Exactly what could he say without passing judgment one way or another? It was not his business.

Back in the barn with buckets of steaming water, with headless, footless chicken corpses submerged, the animals reigned. Flies buzzed, thick around chicken parts, the horses whinnied, and the cow moaned because she had not yet been milked.

"Pluck it clean," Joe said to David.

"When you going to milk the cow?"

"Let the bitch suffer."

Joe wanted David to go, and he wouldn't say anything more unless he had to. "Pull out the gullet," and later,

"Don't be afraid of getting your hands dirty," and finally, "Take one home. Have it for dinner."

"No, it'll be a long time before I eat chicken again," David said as he left.

He's gone, Joe thought, and he'd better not come back for a long time. He'd better not come back to spy on my life. I hate it when he comes around here.

Later, Sheila walked a mile up the road where she'd parked the car, walked into the kitchen without knocking, and they grabbed hold of each other, and he smothered his face in her neck, and he snorted.

Drawing Fishes

Maryanne was sure her watercolor fishes accurately resembled the speckled trout and the blue gill of native waters, but she castigated her pastel rendering of a barracuda because she'd never seen one.

Genevieve, one of her closest friends, said, "What difference does it make if it looks like a fish or a shoe horn? If you say it's a fish, it's a fish." But Maryanne didn't buy that and promised herself that she'd make it a point to see a barracuda if she ever got to a marine world in any major metropolitan area.

Anyway, she might give up fishes and take up onions. Gram Evans said she was crazy, but she went down to the root cellar and brought up the Vidalias.

"You can always eat them so they won't go to waste," she said.

"I always eat what I paint," Maryanne said.

"You get that practical streak from my side of the family, although it skipped a generation with your mother. At least your fish look like fish. You could be painting women with three-nostrilled noses."

Maryanne's shoulders slumped. When would she ever be able to paint something that didn't look like the something she was trying to paint? At least she was trying. She had been getting to the point that her lines blurred, and some of the colors she used couldn't be found in nature; but anyone could see that it was a fish she was trying to paint.

On another visit, her friend Genevieve said she was wasting her time depicting material things and should instead try something abstract like love, or stupidity. She proffered that a painting might start with a swath of red bleeding down the canvas to represent all the bloodshed in all the stupid silly wars. Anyone who saw it would know that it was stupidity she was trying to represent.

"I'll draw my next largemouth bass cross eyed," Maryanne said. "That'll look pretty stupid."

Meanwhile, a pike watercolor and a three-paneled drawing of a muskellunge won blue ribbons at the county fair, and Maryanne got a call from the editor of *Pennsylvania Outdoorsman*, a nature quarterly, asking if he could use the musky panels in an upcoming issue devoted to game fishing.

Maryanne was flattered. Even Gram Evans approved. "I used to say your mother was wrong to encourage you. A woman's got to think about practical things like getting married and having babies. But I'm beginning to think all them fish sketches might pay off. Lord knows, you're pushing 30 and you've never even had a date."

"Gram!"

The picture caused a stir in town, got framed and hung on the post office bulletin board. A few townsfolk called around to look at the original, and two of the town's wealthiest citizens—the accountant and the County Clerk —commissioned small sketches.

When the next year rolled around, *Pennsylvania Outdoorsman* put out a boating issue and commissioned three more drawings, including the likeness of a perch lure.

Ed Ames, the proprietor of Ames's, a store that sold canned goods and live bait, asked Maryanne if he could print some of her drawings on postcards and split the profits after expenses. Gram Evans approved of that, too. "I'm getting less and less concerned about you. I'm the only relative you got left in the world, you never had a steady job, no man's ever tried to catch you, and God knows why your mother encouraged you, but I'm starting to be real pleased," she said.

Maryanne, however, was getting glum. Genevieve had made another visit. "What's happened to you? You were getting to the point where your fish almost didn't look like fish but retained the essence of fish. Then you sold out."

Gram Evans wasn't pleased when next day Maryanne asked her once again for the onions.

"Go ahead and paint onions, you fool. Paint potatoes and winter squash, too, there's enough of them down there."

Maryanne wept.

Maryanne's second onion period was fraught with frustration after it became apparent to her that all her onions looked like people.

Genevieve said, "If you say they're onions, they're onions. You can say they're fish, too, if you want. You're the artist!"

"But they're not fish. They're not even onions!"

"Gram Evans is right. You are practical. Maybe too practical to be an artist."

"Maybe I don't want to be an artist anymore," Maryanne said.

"Maybe you shouldn't be," Genevieve said, spitefully.

In the autumn, when Gram Evans took sick, the proprietor of Ames's brought out a spiral-bound calendar of Maryanne's best sketches, depicting the bullhead, the last she drew before switching to onions. Gram Evans, on her deathbed, managed some consoling words.

"Go back to the fishes, honey."

"I've given them up for good, Gram."

"If they put me into a home, they'll be nothing for you to inherit. You can't support yourself. Go back to the fishes."

"But Gram . . . "

"No buts about it." Gram Evans said and closed her eyes, falling into a deep, deep sleep.

Maryanne, leaving her grandmother's side, took her troubles down to the lake with her lunch packed in a fishing creel. She rowed to the white lilies in the channel, dropped anchor, and ate her cheese sandwich. When she finished, she laid back, rested her head on the seat, closed her eyes, and listened to the water lapping at the side of the boat.

"Maryanne," she in her half sleep heard Gram Evans whisper. "Maryanne. I'm with the Vidalias."

As Maryanne bolted upright scanning both shores for Gram Evans, a bass leapt over the side of the boat and into the open creel.

"Jesus," Maryanne said. "I'm going back to the fishes."

The World Could Have Been Different

"The world could have been different," said the short bald man as he tried tossing a ping pong ball into one of many small goldfish bowls. It, too, slipped between bowls, as had all the others.

"You want to try again?" asked the carnival barker.

"Nah. What do I need a goldfish for anyway?"

"That's what we all say, sooner or later, when we look back with regret," said Louise, another patron.

"No, I mean it," the fat man said, looking straight into her eyes. "The world could have been completely different."

"I don't getchya."

"Listen, if God hadn't thrown Adam and Eve out of the Garden of Eden, humans would have become different."

"Oh, I get it. You're a religious fanatic," Louise said, looking more at the space beside him than at him.

"Didn't you ever stop to think about that?" the fat man asked her.

At that moment, a group of teenage girls bellied up to the railing, squeezing the fat gentleman closer to Louise.

"I didn't come to the fair to talk about religion," she said. "That's the last thing I want to talk about here, or anywhere. And especially at the beer tent, which is where I'm going, mister."

"I'm not talking religion, I'm talking fact."

"Buddy, if you're not going to play, move on," said the barker, eying the two characters up and down. "You know, you two make a lovely couple. Why don't you take a trip down the tunnel of love?" The remark made the girls giggle.

"We're not together," Louise said.

"Like I says, if you're not gonna play . . . "

"Oh, I'm going to play," the fat man said, squinting at the barker through four puffy eyelids. "And I'm going to clean you out of goldfish, too."

"Yeah. Right."

"It's been nice talking to you, but I've got to meet my sister," Louise said.

"I'm telling you that the whole world could have been different," he persisted.

"I don't know about that," she said, tossing her last ball, which bounced off the lip of a bowl and exactly into the outstretched hand of the barker.

"For that, I'm going to let you try again."

"I know my world could have been different if my husband hadn't died," she posited. "And if there hadn't been a Hitler, we wouldn'ta had no World War II."

"That's not what I mean," he said. "I mean, if God hadn't kicked Adam and Eve out of the Garden of Eden, humans would have become different."

The fat man tossed a ball that fell short of even the first row of bowls and onto the sawdust floor.

"Wimp," said one of the giggling girls standing next to him.

"OK, I'll bite," Louise said. "But let's get our facts straight. Things would have been different had Adam and Eve not eaten that apple."

"Well, I don't know about that. You couldn't know human beings very well to say that."

"And you do?"

"Oh, yes."

"But wait a minute," Louise said. "We're like we are, so the story goes, as a result of what they did, right?"

"You're quibbling, but you're also missing my point. Had Adam and Eve not been kicked out of the Garden, human beings would have become a different race of beings."

"Where you gettin' this stuff?" she asked.

"Don't you read your Bible?"

"Uh-oh. He's talking about religion," said one of the giggling girls to her friends. "Let's get outta here." And the four of them melted into the crowd near the tilt-o-whirl.

"You're scaring away my customers," the barker said.

"It's a free country," the fat man said.

"Play or leave."

"I'm not going anywhere until I win something."

"I think it's time to meet my sister," Louise said.

"I thought you weren't supposed to meet your sister until 8:30?"

"Did I say that? Well, you got me. So, how could Adam and Eve have been different?"

"Finally, you've asked the question I wanted you to ask," he said, his two plump cheeks pulling back to reveal a smile that almost swallowed his face.

"I'll bet you'd make a good Santa Claus," she said.

"I've been him. But you're changing the subject. God kicked Adam and Eve out of the Garden of Eden so they wouldn't eat of the Tree of Life and be as gods— immortal!"

Suddenly, the sound of scraping metal pierced the air, and then a scream, followed by many screams, and then a crash.

"Oh, my God," Louise said. "What was that?"

Momentarily, the ball throwing stopped, and many of the patrons walked at once toward the commotion. The fat man took his handful of balls and threw them all at once while closing his eyes. When he opened them, he scanned the tops of the colored water expectantly.

"Sorry, bub. You missed again."

"Not one?"

"Not one."

"What rotten luck."

A siren went off, and more people moved toward the hubbub.

"What happened?" the barker shouted to the Win-go concessionaire across the alley. By now, only the fat man and Louise stood in the sawdust by the railing.

"The Ferris wheel. The pins came out and one of the cars dropped."

"The Ferris wheel?" the fat man said. "Didn't you say you were supposed to meet your sister at 8:30 at the Ferris wheel?"

"Oh, my God," she said. "What time is it?"

"8:38," said the barker.

My All-Seeing Eye

The entire town snores without a single resident waking up to pee or to spread mayonnaise on two slices of bread. Several sleepers, however, roll over, coming out of a dream and into blackness.

Then—imagine the worst possible scenario: your father is being gagged and his hands tied behind his back, and you are unable to scream—Ernest Jones comes out of this dream, sweating and thrashing, accidentally slapping Mrs. Jones awake.

"What it is? What is it?" Mrs. Jones asks as Mr. Jones curls himself into a ball, turning his back toward her. "You've had that dream again," she says, peering over his head and wiping a tear from his eye. He nods his head, and she presses her breasts to his back and her hips to his buttocks and wraps her arms around his chest.

Others awaken. One of the Lake children empties his bladder. Elma Lansbury debates whether to go downstairs to make a chicken sandwich. Dwane Anderson swigs the rest of the coffee royale he left before he passed out. Four minutes and twenty seconds elapse.

The wind blows up South Street, a semi speeds down Route 60, and Mr. Jones slips the stub of this tongue into Mrs. Jones's mouth. As Mrs. Jones unsnaps his pajama bottoms, he lightly runs his fingers down the underside of her arm, clamps his hand around her wrist, and gently forces her over. He sits on her abdomen and looks inquiringly at her. "No, I want to tie you," she says. He shakes his head, no, and takes the rope out of the top dresser drawer where he keeps the note pads that he uses to communicate.

By now, the others have fallen back to sleep. I smile, knowing I can tell you the exact position of every resident. In fact, I can draw the composition of their dreams and I can imitate the noises that they make. But that is not why I am writing. Nor is it my intention to titillate the sexually frustrated. No more will be said of the Joneses. I am merely exercising my all-seeing eye, and ogling the show.

The Plight of the Modern Writer

Today is one of those days when I believe there is nothing more to be written, when all the good subjects have been exhausted, when the best cannot be bettered, when the power of the written word is powerless, when even the language itself seems degenerate. To my mind, no one is worthy of elevated diction, nor is it worth the effort to cleverly bastardize diction in order to elevate the anti-hero.

I think of the two hundred or so families in my hometown that at one time were customers on my paper route. Does the illiterate woman who took a subscription merely for my companionship deserve more than a line of prose? Or the man sauntering in the Victorian evening gown that I espied through his front porch window? Or the richest and most respectable adulterer? I suppose I could elaborate, but I take a very bored and shallow breath.

It is my own life's story that deserves scrutiny: the well-mannered boy who learned to read at the age of two, who composed sonnets at the age of eleven, who read the works of Shakespeare at the age of twelve, who was nicknamed "jobby" at 15 because of his entrepreneurship, who traveled to Europe at 17, who had a crisis of confidence at 19, who became an alcoholic at 22. Imagine all this from the son of a welder and of a chambermaid.

Are you yawning, too? Perhaps one incident can jar you from your *ennui*. I come home, the local boy-made-good, the recovering alcoholic, the only college graduate in the extended family, the Fifth Avenue success story. The family and a few friends discuss astrology and I debunk it, calling it medieval, a tradition passed from the ignorant to the ignorant. I tell an encapsulated history of the western world, emphasizing the church's monopoly on knowledge. My mother beams.

We speak of myths, and someone suggests Jesus' existence is fact because there is a seed of truth to all myths. I explain how myths begin, how the notion of perfection could become personified, how a story might come to be passed on and then exaggerated. They are in awe.

We speak of death, and someone remarks that there must be life after death because all religions have come to that conclusion. I say to them, if a thousand people cannot be wrong, does that mean one person cannot be right? I present in evidence the billions who have died as proof that there is no heaven. I asseverate that so-called proofs of the afterlife are always second-hand, and that the natural instinct for self-preservation is behind all such systems of belief. They say nothing, which I take as affirmation I am right.

Finally, we speak of war, of pollution, of disease, and I am eloquent. All organisms, I say, large or small, must die. I hold a moldy orange before them as a metaphor to the earth, and I liken the mold to human habitation. I propose the end is near.

Do I have you then? Am I not worthy to be a writer? Should I not be filled with proper subjects for literature? Is it any wonder I would not be read? Can you see why it is no use writing?

The World Is Too Much With Us

Humans thought of the world's imminent demise with lengthy and burdensome speculation, depressing civilization like mass displacing water. To the universe, the destruction measured an infinity less than a second.

Nearly a millennium prior to the actual cessation of life on earth, scientists were working on the theory that the sun was to undergo a cataclysmic event. By poking instruments into the changeable crust, by raising telescopes above the atmosphere, by dispatching satellites on voyages into the sun, it was confirmed.

Heads of State were the first to know, but the news erupted and spread like lava among the earth's twenty-three billion inhabitants. Sordid boons: suicide, homicide, genocide.

Years passed. Increasingly, writers wrote bleak adjectives, artists painted fiery lands of desolation, music reeked of brass and percussion. Martial Law was initiated to quell the hysteria.

Soon the sun finished its hydrogen core, proton-proton reactions ceased, the chromosphere collapsed and burned, and the sun expanded to become a red giant which encompassed the earth. The gaseous atmospheres of the major planets dissolved, revealing rocky cores; electric storms announced water, and Proteus, rising from a Jovian sea, and Triton, with his wreathed horn, ushered life in golden chariots.

You Will Know Happiness

I know perfectly well that the world is coming to an end but that has not prevented me from enjoying it. Like everyone else, I have had my share of bad dreams, such as seeing a tree extirpate its roots and wrap its leafy arms around my neck. That was one of the mild ones. But through meditation, I have been able to transcend the impending tragedy and divorce myself from the truth, and, if that is wrong, God help the realist, and God help me, perhaps, because their sidelong glances terrify me.

For now I shall let it go, yes, shall let it all go and create once again the forest as it was, the oaks on the slope and the maples on the crest of the hill, and, yes, it shall be spring, before the leaves have fully bloomed and shaded the sunlight, before the last white trilliums have turned brown, before the last violets have lost their fragrance, before the biting Mayflies have died. The air will have the freshness of my youth, and the dark places its mystery, and I will be small beside the trunks. I will flail the flies from my eyes and hurry through the young maples and sit crying upon a stump to make them go away.

Dear reader, this picture has not been an easy one to reconstruct. It has taken me nearly thirty years to do so, and each time it is at once clearer and more unreal, as if a man, whose blindness was not congenital, were trying to remember the color yellow. Oh, that is precisely right, because not only has youth fled, which is the universal, but so has this patch of woods or any like it, which is the particular.

I am not trying to be a prophet of doom, for prophets appear before an age, and I am not even stating the facts because the facts have been stated. I am trying to teach the reader the only means left to pure happiness, and, sadly, it can no longer occur in the present, in the World of Now.

Yes, there are yet trilliums left in the full of their bloom, and violets with their richest fragrance. I pick up a twig that has blown from a treetop and examine the light green budding leaves and the wrinkles of youth. It is not with my arms, but with this twig that I brush the biting flies from the corners of my eyes, and I am standing on the stump on the crest of the hill, and I am king of the world.

I have had other dreams and I shall repeat the one that repeats itself most often. I am drawn into a rotted hole in the trunk of a tree on the promise of treasure and, finding one inside, am barred from exiting as the tree squeezes in and my arms become its arms and likewise my skin its bark, and the lumberman cannot hear my shouts. Do you understand?

As many times as I have awakened from its throes, I would rather have this nightmare than the one my neighbors have had in which their flesh is seared from their bones and they are silently screaming. And yet they envy the placidity of my dreams. You can have them, but I am instructing you privately, and not to your face, because

I will not again be accused of insanity or insensitivity. I am not happy we are suffering.

Again, I see the oak that I cannot completely embrace, and the maple sapling I am as tall as. I have one pure handful of odorless trilliums and one pure handful of fragrant violets and with these I whisk away the biting flies as the petals fall. But I must protect the perfection of the flowers. How can I do so without mixing the flowers? I hop from stump to stump giggling.

I must point out my woodland meditation is not a dream, although when happiness could be found in the World of Now it would have been called a daydream. "But you are a very old man," I recall being said, "and you are lucky to remember such things." It is not impossible to teach a congenitally blind man the color yellow, though I admit it is a difficult task because it must be done by telling him what yellow is not, which is an infinite process in a finite world. It is, however, worth the effort of the last few generations to learn.

I urge you to read between the paragraphs the world that is not there. You will find happiness.